The Spotted Cottage by the Sea

AN Press

Pittsburgh

THE SPOTTED COTTAGE BY THE SEA

ANJ Press, First edition. March 2024.

Copyright © 2024 Amelia Addler.

Written by Amelia Addler.

Cover design by Lori Jackson

https://www.lorijacksondesign.com/

Maps by MistyBeee

for Tokitae

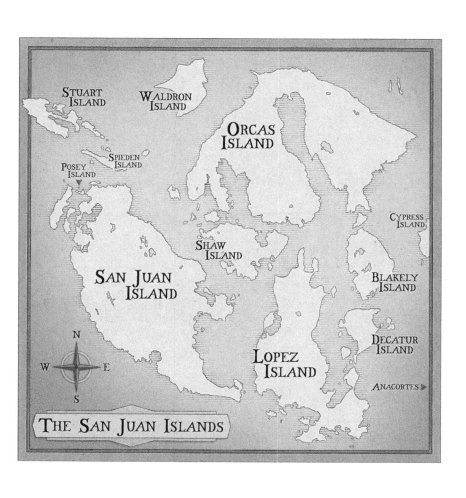

STUART
ISLAND

WALDRON
ISLAND

ORCAS
ISLAND

SPIEDEN
ISLAND

POSEY
ISLAND

CYPRESS
ISLAND

SHAW
ISLAND

SAN JUAN
ISLAND

BLAKELY
ISLAND

DECATUR
ISLAND

N
W — E
S

LOPEZ
ISLAND

ANACORTES ▶

THE SAN JUAN ISLANDS

One

S heila never needed anyone's help, and getting herself fired that morning was no exception. All it took was one out-of-place box.

Her kids liked to joke about her love of boxes. Their house was impeccably organized with them – long, flat boxes tucked under beds, stuffed with out-of-season clothes; clear plastic boxes stacked in the pantry, filled with rice or cereal or sugar; wicker boxes in the mud room, mostly empty, but there to complete the aesthetic.

The girls' Christmas presents were never in bags, but instead in beautiful, patterned boxes wrapped exquisitely with ribbon. Sheila would stay up until three in the morning getting the hand-made bows *just* right.

So, of course, when the special corrugated pink bakery box she'd ordered came as a set of two, she couldn't let one go to waste.

She filled the first box with her homemade donuts, as planned, neatly layering and dusting them with powdered sugar.

The second box was never part of the plan – any plan – but it was so perfect, so sturdy, she filled it with the potential solution to her longest-held problem. It was a secret she'd had for decades; it was the story her mind went to with every inane corporate icebreaker, but the one story she never could—nor did—tell.

Keeping them both in the trunk of her car had seemed logical at the time. She didn't want the secret box to accidentally be discovered in the house. Though the girls had all moved out – her youngest just a few weeks ago, off to college – they could pop in at any moment and be tempted by the promise of baked goods.

No, the car was the right place to hide it, and that morning, in the parking lot at work, she threw the trunk open and butterflies took off in her stomach.

"How awful would it be if I picked up the wrong box?" Sheila thought to herself.

She laughed and laughed, then leaned over and did just that.

It was unfortunate. It wasn't the sort of day to get fired, the lazy Tuesday after a holiday, the air sharp and cool, a relief from the heaviness of the recent heat wave. Labor Day had brought rain and the city breathed a collective sigh of relief, opening its windows to the wide cerulean skies.

Sheila loved Seattle in the fall, and even more so here in Lynnwood, which she referred to as Seattle to non-natives, though it was a little more north and a little less glamorous. It was where she'd raised her kids, where she'd watched her life crack to pieces, and where she'd found the strength to put it back together again.

This was her final act. These donuts were the *key*.

She stood and took a deep breath, savoring the moment. Accounting wasn't the most glamorous profession, she'd admit, but she was good at it. So good they'd promoted her right up to now, when she'd show them she deserved to be a senior manager.

The new office would be nice. The raise would be appreciated. But what she desperately needed was the bonus.

She'd never admit this to anyone, but she was broke. It was a miracle she'd made it this far, budgeting and scrimping to raise four daughters in the Seattle metro area, but she'd finally run out of tricks. The mortgage was overdue – the second mortgage was overdue, too – and this bonus was her only hope to pull herself out of disaster.

Life was expensive, especially with an ex-husband who thought the girls didn't deserve any help while they were studying. He had a new family to maintain, after all.

Sheila stood and straightened her shoulders. She told herself being broke didn't mean she was a bad accountant. Even if she didn't believe it.

It would all be okay. This was the final step to fix *everything*.

A familiar voice snapped her out of thoughts. "You're all loaded up. Let me help you."

It was Amy, her friend and next-door-cubicle mate.

Sheila smiled and shook her head. "I'm all right, but thanks."

"Oh, come on, give me something!" She reached for the bag straps on Shelia's shoulder and started to pry.

Sheila shimmied away. "Ah, stop. Fine! You can take the box."

The box, pink and perfect in every way, except for what was inside of it.

A smile spread across Amy's face. "What's in here?"

"Donuts." That was, at least, what she thought.

Amy tilted her head. "These are some heavy donuts. All for me?"

Sheila laughed and struggled against the straps of the bags as she shut the trunk. "Of course. I made them myself."

"What!" Amy tried to lift the corner of the box, but it was taped shut. "When did you have time to do that?"

They strode, side by side, through the front doors of the building and called the elevator. "This morning. They had to be fresh. That's what Dan taught me."

Amy narrowed her eyes. "Dan? Is that your new boyfriend? Did you get a hit on a dating app?"

Sheila laughed. "Yeah, right. What would I even put in my profile? *Single mom. Music taste stuck in the 90's. Doing my best. Bad at it.*"

"*Makes donuts,*" Amy added. "For Dan, at least."

They got out of the elevator and Sheila lowered her voice. "It's not just any Dan. It was CEO of Dan's Donuts *Dan.*"

Amy stopped in her tracks. "Don't tell me you landed the Dan's Donuts account."

A smile tore across Sheila's face. "Last month he gave me a donut recipe, and after about a thousand practice donuts, I finally got it right. I showed up with a dozen of them and he said I knew the business and he'd love to work with me."

Amy squealed. "Sheila, that's insane! They're almost as big as Dunkin' Donuts!"

"Don't let Dan hear you say that," she said with a smile. "In his mind, they already are."

As far as she was concerned, they were, too. Her biggest account ever. The donuts that would save her house.

Amy picked at the tape on the box. "I guess I can't have any until the partners, managers, seniors and whatever interns are at the meeting get their cut, then?"

Sheila reached for the box and snapped the tape open. "Of course not. Take one!"

Amy slammed her hand on the lid and shut it. "No, I'll wait. We'll get coffee after and you can tell me all about it. Should I put this in the conference room?"

"Sure. Thank you."

Later, when Sheila ruminated on these fateful moments, she would tell herself there were so many chances where she could have figured out it was the wrong box.

Of course, her greatest mistake was accepting help. If she'd carried the box herself, she would have noticed it was the wrong one.

Instead, she merrily went to the conference room and set up her presentation, then watched as everyone slowly filled the seats around the conference table.

The seat at the head of the table was saved for CEO Anthony Silva. He came in five minutes past the hour, chatting and shaking hands before sitting down.

He wasn't a man she interacted with often – not yet at least. That would all change after her promotion. After she dropped the bomb of landing a huge account.

Sheila closed the door just as Anthony took notice of the pink box in center of the table.

"Ah. Is this for me?" he asked, pulling the box closer.

"Yes, I made them. And I'm making you a deal," Sheila said. "A deal you can't refuse."

Muted laughter made its way around the table, and Anthony smiled before popping the lid of the box open.

Some might think accountants shouldn't have a flair for the dramatic, but Sheila didn't agree with that. She clicked the computer alive and a six-foot tall image of herself in front of the local Dan's Donuts projected onto the screen.

Anthony looked up at her. "Is this some sort of joke?"

She stood next to her picture, grinning. "I don't joke about dough!"

He pushed the box away and stood. "Call security." He buttoned his suit jacket and jerked his head in Sheila's direction. "Get her out of here."

Sheila stared, the smile frozen on her face as the realization dawned on her that maybe, just *maybe*, she may have done exactly what she'd feared.

She rushed over, ripped the lid open, and gasped.

Inside was a black rope, a ski mask, gloves, wire cutters, rappelling gear, and a lock picking kit.

It was, undeniably, the wrong box.

Two

I t wasn't fair to bother Sheila with her problems. Patty knew she only had herself to blame. She was eighty years old, for goodness' sake! She should've known better.

Sheila had her own life. Her hands were full. Patty wasn't going to bother her.

Except...there was one problem. Derby. Not that *he* was a problem – a darling Golden Retriever who loved everyone could never be a problem. But he couldn't come with her, and who but Sheila would want a ten-year-old dog with arthritic hips and one deaf ear?

Patty sighed. The price of aging with grace.

She stared at her phone. Though Sheila was technically her *ex*-daughter-in-law, there wasn't much ex about her. She was the mother of her precious grandchildren. She called three times a week just to chat, and when Patty's husband Ray had died, it was Sheila who planned the funeral, only days after being handed divorce papers by Patty's own son.

The divorce. Just when Patty thought her heart couldn't get broken into smaller pieces, Brian had decided he wanted a divorce. Patty would never understand why.

Sheila survived it, though, and survived raising four teenaged daughters. She could surely handle taking in one aging Golden Retriever.

Patty hit the call button, and it rang twice before she rushed to hang up.

No. She couldn't tell Sheila about any of this until it was over. A done deal. Until she was halfway across the country.

Telling Sheila now would only make things worse. She'd try to fix everything. She'd insist there was something they could do when there most certainly was not.

Her phone lit up with a picture of Sheila's smiling face.

Oops. Apparently, she hadn't hung up soon enough.

Patty cleared her throat and answered. "Hey, sweetheart."

"Is everything okay, Patty?" Sheila asked. "You don't normally call me in the middle of the morning."

"Everything is great," she lied. "How are you? How's Emma doing with her first week at school? Did she come home for the weekend?"

Sheila laughed. "No, of course not. She couldn't wait to leave the nest. I'll be lucky to get them all home for Thanksgiving."

Patty's smile faded. Thanksgiving. She would miss that, too, for the first time ever. Would she be alone for it? Would Brian take pity on her and visit the retirement home, or would he jet off to the Caribbean with his new bride and stepsons?

"You know what?" Sheila added. "I was just thinking I needed to pay you a visit. It's been too long."

A year, but who was counting? After Ray's memorial, Patty couldn't deal with visitors. She was too embarrassed by her grief, and by the time she was ready, a virus had overtaken the world.

That was when her troubles really began. She had broken her hip and ended up away from home and her beloved tea shop for *months*.

Sheila came to help, of course, but Patty was able to gloss over issues with the tea shop. The focus then was on her health, which annoyingly refused to return with the speed she wanted.

When Patty got back home, she couldn't move quite like she used to, but she figured she'd sort it out once the world opened up again. She thought the tea shop would eventually bounce back. She thought *she* would bounce back.

As it happens, there isn't much bouncing at eighty, and a tea shop that was closed for the better part of five years needed a lot of work to reopen.

"Sure," Patty said weakly, "stop by any time."

Sheila was quiet for a moment. "You sound winded. Are you okay?"

"Yes."

"You don't sound okay."

This was silly. She just needed to say it.

Patty took a deep breath and steadied her voice. "I am fine, thank you. You are welcome to visit, but I'm afraid it might be your last visit to San Juan Island. At least with me here."

"What?" Sheila's voice boomed through the phone. "What happened? What's wrong?"

Patty took a seat on the worn recliner in her living room. She'd set it up facing the large bay windows overlooking the water. It was her favorite view on earth, and she would miss it terribly.

This house had been her and Ray's dream. They bought it in retirement, and Ray's handiness led them to repair the old building on the property and turn it into a darling tea shop.

The one that was now locked and surely coated in inches of dust. Patty's chest swelled with shame when she thought of it, but she didn't know what to do. Nothing had gone according to plan. Ray would be disappointed in her, but at the same time, he wasn't supposed to die and leave her to take care of it on her own.

"Life happened, Sheila. I'm not asking for your pity, and I'm not asking for your help." She paused. "Derby will need you, though."

"My word, Patty. Are you sick?"

She chuckled. "No. I'm just old. I've decided it's time for my next step."

"Your next step?" Sheila laughed. "What are you going on about? I told you you're too old to join the circus again."

That simply wasn't true, but she wasn't going to argue. "I talked to Brian and he found a place for me."

"You already have a place, Patty?"

She cleared her throat. "He found a place closer to him. Closer to New York City."

"I bet he did," Sheila spat. "What about the tea shop? You can't be ready to give that up."

"Who said anything about giving it up? I'm moving on, Sheila. On and up!" She forced a smile. She could believe it if she faked believing it. Maybe. "I just can't take Derby with me. Will you take him in? Give him the golden years he deserves?"

"Absolutely not. I'm coming up to see you. I'm buying a ferry ticket as we speak." There were tapping sounds, then, "Looks like I'll have to leave my car on the mainland. There aren't any reservations. But you'll pick me up, won't you Patty?"

"Don't be ridiculous," Patty said. "Don't you have to work? You can't drop everything and come up here. This is why I didn't tell you in the first place."

"I don't have work. I just got fired. So I'm free for..." She paused, drawing out a "Hm," then added, "forever."

"Ha ha. Very funny," Patty said. "I do not want to see you here, Sheila. I will not pick you up from the ferry."

"I'll be there in three hours. I'm bringing donuts."

Baffled, Patty pulled the phone away from her ear. "Sheila? Do not come here! You are not welcome!"

But Sheila was already gone, calling her bluff.

Three

The announcement for walk-on passengers to board the ferry rang out. Sheila picked up her box and started moving, keeping her eyes fixed on the sparkling water beneath the ferry.

This time, she had the right box. She was sure of it. The burglary box, as Amy called it, had stayed behind in her car in the ferry parking lot.

Dear, kind Amy. She had tried to save Sheila's job – she really did. As an HR director, she had a lot of experience in smoothing things over and a lot of tricks up her sleeve. She pulled out every one.

Her first attempt was saying the items in the box were for rock climbing, but the ski mask made it a tough sell.

Then she suggested it was poorly thought-out joke, not worth losing a star accountant over. Unfortunately, the CEO had suffered three break-ins and a slew of threatening notes in the past year, so he didn't find it funny.

Sheila walked into the quiet passenger cabin of the ferry. There were the familiar fluorescent lights, the linoleum floors, and blue pleather booths. Wide windows spanned the entire length of the cabin, where astounding views of the islands contrasted with the drab interior of the ship.

It hadn't changed one bit. Even the posters on the walls look the same as the last time she'd been here, as though frozen in time.

Sheila didn't have that luxury. She didn't get to stay the same. She didn't even get a pause button.

The Sheila who used to ride on this ferry had been happily married. She and Brian and the kids bought sweets from the galley and marveled at the view from the windows, the islands rising from the foggy mists like ghosts over the water.

Perhaps Sheila had a ghost, too. One who still rode this ferry. A carefree Sheila, one who had no idea what dark nights lay ahead.

She *wished* she could still be that Sheila. She never even got the chance to say goodbye! One day, Brian decided he was in love with someone else and that Sheila was gone, replaced with a harried woman who had to find a way to hold it all together.

She flopped into a seat and stared at the pink box in front of her. Intellectually, she knew she should feel embarrassed over her firing, or at least worried. Instead, all she felt was anger.

She'd earned that promotion, burglary box or not. Every year, they had told her there wasn't room in the budget, so every year she kept working harder.

What choice did she have? She'd had to spend everything to buy out Brian's portion of the house in the divorce. He didn't make it easy, because just like with his mother now, he thought everyone would benefit from following him to New York. He'd expected the girls to leave the only home they'd ever known to become a blended family with his new lover and her kids.

Thinking about it got her angry all over again. He'd gone off and had the most cliché mid-life crisis to "find" himself and emerged even more self-centered than before.

When did Sheila get to find herself? When did she even get a moment to stop and breathe?

She looked up from the box as the other passengers filed in – families with kids, young-and-in-love couples, and groups of college-aged students. One particularly rowdy group of young men walked in her direction, laughing and roughhousing in the aisle.

Just as they passed Sheila, one of the guys took another in a headlock. He protested, thrashing against his captor and dumping an entire cup of hot chocolate directly onto Sheila's chest.

She let out a shriek and tugged the burning material from her skin.

"You spilled my drink, man!" the boy yelled, and they disappeared around the corner without ever looking back.

"Don't mind me," Sheila muttered. "How rude of me to absorb your drink."

A middle-aged woman with soulful eyes rushed over. "Oh goodness! Are you all right?"

Sheila waved a hand. "Oh yes, I'm fine. Just a bit of a mess."

"I'll get some napkins!"

"No, thank you, but it's okay. There's already a stack here." Sheila cleared her throat. Hopefully the woman hadn't heard her grumbling to herself.

The woman put her hands on her hips. "What about a new shirt? I'm sure I can get something from the lost and found."

As unappealing as an old stranger's shirt was, Sheila hadn't brought any spare clothes, and the sticky-sweet smell of the chocolate on her skin was making her sick.

"Ah...sure. That's very kind of you."

She took off and reappeared not five minutes later with a black T-shirt in her hand. At the top was a yellow moon and around it were three howling wolves. "I think this'll be a bit big for you, but it'll do the job."

"Thank you." She accepted the shirt. "I'm Sheila, by the way."

"Margie! Pleased to meet you." She extended a handshake. "Are you new to the island?"

"Not exactly. I'm going to see my mother-in-law, Patty Dennet."

Margie gasped. "I know Patty! She's a doll. Well, I'll let you get dressed, and maybe I'll see you on the island?"

Sheila smiled. Of course they knew each other. "Sure. See you around!"

If memory served her right, there was a bathroom around the corner where she could change. Sheila disappeared and returned to her things untouched.

Back in her seat, she pulled out the book she'd been struggling through for weeks but, as always, her mind wandered.

Had she even needed to leave to get dressed? It wasn't like anyone was looking at her. She was a middle-aged woman, which meant she was, for all intents and purposes, invisible.

She looked up from her book and saw that a man was looking at her. He was in the booth in front of her, and his light blue eyes were locked in.

Sheila blinked. He was handsome, strikingly so. He had wide shoulders under a soft-looking green flannel shirt, a salt-and-pepper beard, and a black baseball cap pulled low over his face.

It was too absurd. She turned, looking over her shoulder to see whoever he was actually looking at, and when she turned back, he was standing at the edge of her booth.

"Hi," he said. "Nice wolves."

Four

The woman peered up at him, her brow furrowed, and her arms crossed over her chest. "I'm sorry?"

Russell motioned to the book now face-down on the table. "Were you reading *The Rise of Wolf 8?*"

"Oh." She picked it up and faced the cover toward him. It did indeed have a wolf on the cover, but the title was *The 8 Wolves Inside You.*

He reached forward. "May I?"

She nodded and slid the book toward him.

He took a seat across from her in the booth and turned the book in his hands. The subtitle was *Embracing your instincts for transformation in midlife.*

"Well, this is embarrassing," he said, handing the book back to her. "I thought you were reading a different book – one by Rick McIntyre."

She raised an eyebrow. "Is he a friend of yours?"

"I wish," he said. "I mean, I've met him. He's a really nice guy, but no. I'm just a hobbyist." He leaned in and lowered his voice. "Between the wolf on your book and the wolves on your shirt, I thought you were a fellow wolf enthusiast."

She looked down at her shirt and laughed. "Oh! Okay, I can see how you might've thought that."

The shirt looked out of place on her; it was what first caught his eye. Maybe she was wearing it ironically? She was pretty, with dark hair framing her delicate features – a small nose tucked between high cheekbones, and freckles dotting her skin. Her deep brown eyes were ever so slightly outlined with makeup.

He let out a dramatic sigh. "And now I've outed myself as a wolf nerd to a perfectly normal person."

She uncrossed her arms. "Thank you for suggesting I'm normal."

He laughed. "I just started tracking wolves recently. I'm not very good at it. I've also done some wolf watching in Yellowstone. That was where Wolf 8 lived."

"Wolf 8," she repeated slowly.

"Yeah. Him and his stepson, Wolf 21."

A half smile formed on her lips. "I can't tell if you're messing with me."

"About which part?"

"Wolves have stepkids?" she asked.

"Yeah! That's what Rick discovered. He spent his career watching wolves. They're remarkable."

Her eyes lingered on his face. She tilted her head to the side. "Do I know you from somewhere?"

Oh boy. There it was. His disguise could only last so long. He needed to grow the beard bigger. Bushier, maybe dye it white like Santa Claus. "Don't think so, no."

She gasped, covering her mouth with her hands. "You're Russell Westwood!"

He flashed a smile and stood from his seat. "Am I?"

"You are. Wait." She dropped her voice to a whisper. "Aren't you?"

Russell put his hands out. "Who knows? Take care!"

Grinning, he walked off toward the doors that opened onto the deck. He pushed them out against the vicious wind blowing and stepped outside.

He probably shouldn't approach strangers in public like that. Russell had never been good at the celebrity part of being an actor. His wife used to say he was the most awkward heart-throb Hollywood had ever known.

Ex-wife. Holly was his *ex*-wife. Just as he was an ex-heart-throb.

He'd have to work on his social skills. Spending his time tracking wolves through the wilderness had done a number on him.

It was part of the reason he'd moved to San Juan Island. He needed to rejoin society, and a secluded island seemed just the place. The risk of him being swarmed by fans or paparazzi was low.

It was a chance to live normally, or somewhat normally, if he could keep himself from getting overly excited by a woman reading a book that wasn't really about wolves.

Outside on the deck, air roared past his ears. He could've used a jacket, but he didn't want to go back down to his car to get one. Instead, he walked to the railing and hung his hands over the side.

Russell loved taking the ferry. It never got old. He loved to stand on the deck as the boat hummed, slow and steady, passing the lush, green-treed islands with their rocky edges.

He stood there for some time before his peace was disturbed at the other end of the deck.

He stared, squinting into the sun, and realized it was two young women blasting music. One of them was performing a dance while the other filmed.

This went on for a minute, then they paused, reviewed the footage, and started again. And again. And again.

Whenever someone walked by, in view of the camera, the performer rolled her eyes, one time throwing her hands up in frustration.

Russell didn't get it. What was the point? It wasn't for fun; it didn't look like fun. It had to be some attempt for fame, if only for the thirty seconds it took to watch the video.

Fame was the intent, the goal, the final destination. Fame without reason, attention for the sake of attention.

It was a tale as old as time. He wished he could tell her she was feeding a bottomless pit. That fame would ruin everything she held dear, strip her life of meaning, and push her loved ones away. It would consume everything and produce nothing. Make her retreat into an empty home, or a snowbank in search of wolves, or an island that could only be reached by ferry or plane.

If there was any chance she'd listen to him, he'd tell her nothing lasts forever. Not fame, not fortune. Not even love.

Those were the sort of things people didn't want to hear, though. He watched a moment longer, then turned to go back inside. That was enough socializing for the day. He'd try again tomorrow.

Five

The ferry made its entrance into the Port of Friday Harbor and Patty peered over her steering wheel, her mind turning. There had to be *something* she could say to Sheila that would work. Something that would convince her to get back on that ferry and go home.

People started streaming off the ferry and she opened her car door, steadying herself on the headrest as she slowly raised herself onto the sidewalk.

Her new hip might be a marvel of modern medicine, but nothing replaced the body of her youth. Oh, how she'd taken it for granted! How amazing it was when everything just worked and her joints didn't ache without reason.

Her eyes worked well enough, though, and she could see Sheila smiling at her from across the street.

Patty raised a hand and waved. She'd have to be firm with her. Tell Sheila it was none of her business what she planned to do with her retirement.

Patty was happy with her life, after all. She had nothing to complain about. She wasn't looking for help, and she most certainly wouldn't be accepting any.

She started walking down the sidewalk as Sheila made her way up. They met on the corner of Front Street, and before

AMELIA ADDLER

Patty could say a word, Sheila dropped her purse and the box she was carrying onto a bench and threw her arms around her. "I can't tell you how much I've missed you."

Patty laughed, hugging her back. "I just saw you for the Fourth of July!"

Sheila pulled away and took a deep breath. "I'm ashamed I haven't been here to see you in so long."

"Don't you start with that." Patty pointed down at the pink box on the bench. "What was it you said about donuts? I thought you were joking."

Sheila laughed, stooping down to grab the box and popping the lid open. "I don't joke about donuts."

They were perfect – golden brown, round, and dusted with sugar. She reached in and took one. "Where did you buy these?"

"I made them."

"Don't you have enough problems? Making donuts, my word." Patty took a bite. There was a crisp snap as she bit in, a hint of vanilla, and of course, the perfect puff of fluffy dough. "This is *wonderful*. But I wouldn't expect any less from you."

"You could sell them in the shop," Sheila mused. "Give me a job."

Without thinking, Patty scoffed. "And pay you with what?"

Sheila leaned down to pick up her purse. "With tea, maybe? I don't know. I don't care. Let me pick the music and you have a deal."

"I'm not hiring," Patty said flatly, starting the walk back to her car. She needed to change the subject. "Do you want to go

24

to the movies? I think there's something with that actor you like."

Sheila drew herself up and followed behind. "What actor?"

"You know, the handsome one." Patty flashed a smile. "Idris Elba. I know how you like him."

"I don't think I've seen him in anything," Sheila said. "I don't want to watch a movie. I want to know what's going on with you."

"We can go for a picnic," Patty continued. "There's a wonderful little shop that opened in town and they sell ready-to-go picnic baskets. I know that you like brie, and they bring in these great big cheese wheels from France –"

"Stop trying to distract me with cheese. It's not going to work." Sheila stopped walking, both feet firmly planted on the sidewalk. "I came here to talk about you. What's going on?"

"Nothing is going on. I just decided to make a change."

Sheila tilted her head. "Oh really? You've decided to move to the New York countryside on your own? It had nothing to do with Brian?"

"I've a mind of my own. Don't start on me with that!" Patty threw her hands up. "You know, Brian had a good point. The cottage and the tea shop are on a beautiful property – ten acres, right on the water. Maybe someone could do something useful with it."

Sheila's mouth fell open. "What do you mean something *useful*? It's your home!" She narrowed her eyes. "Is Brian trying to convince you to sell? Is that what this is about?"

"Selling is a *responsible* idea, Sheila."

"Since when have you been responsible?"

Patty looked at her watch. "You know, if we hurry, there still might be something left at the bakery. I like their croissants. Terrible for my blood sugar, but wonderful for my soul."

Patty turned and kept walking until she reached her car. She opened the driver's side door and waited for Sheila to catch up.

"Patty." She pulled the back door open and dumped her things inside. "You're the one who tried to convince us to quit our jobs when we had a one-year-old and move to the Fiji Islands with you."

"That was a *great* opportunity!" She shook her head. "I don't think you would've liked the bugs, though."

"You lived on a cruise ship for a year. You once traded your minivan for a motorcycle. Since when have you been concerned about being responsible?"

Patty stuck her nose into the air. "Maybe I think it'll be a fun change! It's like joining the circus again, except all the performers are old like me."

She got into the driver's seat and started the car. Sheila got in next to her and buckled her seat belt.

Patty cleared her throat. "Of course, I would split the money. Half to you, and half to Brian."

Sheila sucked in a deep breath, her lips growing tight and pale, her eyes narrowed. When she spoke again, her voice was a whisper. "I do not need money, and neither does Brian."

Now she'd done it. If she could've planned what to say to upset Sheila the most, that was it. "Can't an old woman have her secrets? Let me ride off into the sunset with my dignity."

Sheila crossed her arms. "If I was worried about your dignity, I would've hired a guy with a tuba to follow you around to play your own personal soundtrack."

Patty tried to keep a straight face, but the image floated into her mind and stuck. She started to laugh, and then Sheila started to laugh, the two of them wailing in the car like fools.

When the moment passed, Patty wiped the tears from her eyes and put the car in drive. "Fine. I'll show you what's happened, you stubborn old mule, and then you'll understand."

Sheila sat back, a smile on her face. "Took you long enough."

Six

They drove east on Turn Point Road, a short six-minute trip through Sheila's memory. The winding roads were unchanged, as were the bowing trees and stunning glimpses of the ocean between the leaves.

How could it have been eighteen years since Patty and Ray told them they'd bought the property? It made no sense. Time never made sense to Sheila anymore; it felt like decades had slipped between her fingers.

Still, it had happened. At the time, Patty and Ray had been working on a cruise ship and the captain, whom Ray had befriended, sold the land to them at a bargain.

"You two young kids have dreams," he'd said.

They were 63 and 62.

It was the year Sheila's youngest, Emma, was born, the year Brian said in no uncertain terms that her returning to work would ruin his career and, subsequently, all their futures.

She could still see the pleading look in his eyes, how he'd bounced little Emma in his arms, desperate to get her to sleep, desperate for any of them to sleep.

Patty made a turn onto her driveway and Sheila could see the cottage in the distance, sitting not a hundred yards from the water. The tea shop was close, just off the driveway, with a small gravel parking lot behind it. It too had a view of the water, and its pea gravel patio stood empty, umbrellas for the tables wrapped and faded from the sun.

Ray had come up with the idea for the tea shop's name – The Briny Brew. As much as Sheila hated it, she had still helped him paint the wooden sign he'd wanted for the front.

Speaking of – it seemed to be missing.

"Did you rename the tea shop?" Sheila asked.

Patty shook her head.

"Where's the sign?" She leaned forward, studying the structure. There were no cars in the parking lot, and it didn't look like any lights were on.

"Are you closed today because I came to visit?" Sheila asked.

Patty kept quiet until she reached the parking spot behind the cottage. She turned off the car with a sigh. "No, honey. It's not because of you."

Before she could ask any more questions, Patty got out of the car.

Sheila followed her and took a closer look at the cottage. It wasn't a large house, though it had always served Patty well. Two stories tall, it had enough bedrooms to cram them all in for birthdays and Christmases and Mother's Day brunches, always with a spectacular view of the sea. When the girls were young, they'd build bonfires on the beach and sit roasting marshmallows under the starlight, and when they had gotten older, Patty insisted on hosting birthdays and graduation parties on the beach.

As warm as her memories of the place were, she could admit this was one area where time hadn't stood still. The cottage's pale sea foam paint had peeled in strips and chunks, exposing the gray wood beneath. Bushes and grasses had overgrown the pathway to the house. Weeds edged every corner, and the little mailbox stood crooked, like it had been knocked over and never put quite right again.

"You can see why Brian was tipped off," Patty said, shaking her head. "A neighbor called him and ratted me out. Told him the house looked abandoned."

"It doesn't look abandoned," Sheila said, her voice going too high to be truthful.

"Don't try to use your kindness on me, Sheila." She sighed. "You know, I've never been obsessive about landscaping or how things *looked*, but this has gotten out of hand, even for me. The neighbor told Brian it looks like a spotted cottage from the water with all the paint peeling off."

Sheila turned to Patty, but her eyes were fixed on the cottage. Surely, she didn't see the weeds or the peeling paint or the drooping roof.

She saw something else – the dreams she and Ray had had together, dreams stolen away when Ray died.

Sheila knew a thing or two about futures being stolen away, about dreams dead and gone. When Brian had told her he wanted a divorce, the perfect plans they'd created vanished overnight.

It made Sheila question everything. Had their life ever been real at all if it could disappear without a trace? It felt like she'd lost her bearing in the world then. She used to have a clear image of her life, of her future. She used to know where she was going. It all disappeared in an instant, on the whim of a man looking for himself.

"So what?" Sheila said. "We need to get someone out here to paint it. Big deal."

Patty turned, her eyes solemn. "And whatever else we can't see. Honestly, I'm afraid to look."

Sheila's heart constricted in her chest. She couldn't let Patty walk away from her home, not like this. Not in defeat. "Aren't you going to invite me in for a cup of tea?"

"All right. One cup, then I'm taking you back to the ferry."

She followed Patty up the walkway, preparing herself for the worst – boxes and dishes stacked to the ceiling, piles of dirty laundry, maybe a wall covered in newspaper clippings with words outlined in red.

But when Patty opened the creaking wooden door, the cottage looked just as cozy as ever. Derby rushed to greet them, his grand golden tail wagging, as he presented a shoe in his mouth, promptly pressing it into Sheila's leg.

She knelt down and he overwhelmed her, knocking her to the ground and dropping the shoe to lick her face.

"Okay, Derby," she yelled. "I thought you were supposed to be an old man!"

"*Derby!* Is this how we treat our guests?" Patty yelled, grabbing him by the collar and dragging him off.

Sheila laughed and sat up, regaining her balance as Derby reached as far as he could to plant another lick on her arm.

"I think he missed you." Patty said, smiling down at them.

Sheila stood and scratched behind Derby's ear. This halted his love attack and he tilted his head to the side, leaning into it.

He had aged, but he was as handsome as ever with his entirely white muzzle and his traditional rounded golden retriever body.

"He's covered in dander. I can't pick him up to put him in the tub anymore for a bath," Patty said. "The groomer I used to go to left the island. That'll be the first thing you do when you take him, okay? You have to give him a bath. Brush him out. He loves to be beautiful."

"Derby has always been a diva." Sheila stood up and dusted the fur off her pants. "I'll give him a bath right here."

Patty rolled her eyes, slowly making her way down the hall and into the kitchen. "I have lavender Earl Gray. Do you still like it?"

"It's my favorite." Sheila took her shoes off and set them aside. The hallway leading to the kitchen still had all the old photographs she remembered: a black-and-white picture of Patty and Ray when they had worked in the circus. Brian as a baby, riding the subway in Tokyo. Pictures of the girls, murals of them, from newborn to graduation day, with Patty smiling proudly in the background.

Patty had been the model grandmother. It was a shame when Brian tried to fire her from her post.

Sheila wouldn't have it, and neither would Patty. She came to stay with them during the difficult months of the divorce, during those dark days when Sheila had to meet with her lawyer again and again, digging her fingernail into the skin on her thumb until she bled. Re-picking and opening the scab, for months and months.

Sheila broke her gaze from the pictures and wandered into the kitchen.

"I apologize for the mess. I've been busy," Patty said, setting teacups on the small kitchen table.

"There's no mess." Sheila took a seat, eyeing the tidy shelves lined with containers of flour and sugar and loose tea. There was a new floor mat by the back door, and a pair of men's boots sat atop it. "Did Brian forget his shoes here?"

Patty's eyes shot over to the mat and her mouth popped open. "Yes. He did."

"How long was he here for?" Sheila stopped herself. "You know what, you don't have to tell me. I'm sorry. I'm not trying to be nosy."

Though of course she *did* wonder – had Brian visited with his new wife? With his new stepchildren, the ones he'd chosen to live with on the other side of the country?

"He didn't visit for long," she said slowly. "He came to check on me and to make inquiries. About the property."

Sheila had clenched her jaw and had to take a deep breath to unclench it. "Has he already found a buyer, then?"

"Oh, Sheila, don't start. Brian's right. I can't live here forever."

"What about the tea shop? If you're having trouble with the business, maybe we can finally rename it and start from there."

"I'm having a lot of trouble with the tea shop." Patty dried her hands on a lemon-printed dish towel and threw it on the counter. "It hasn't been open in years, Sheila. After I broke my hip, it was just too hard to manage. My employees left the island because they couldn't afford to live here, then something happened with the insurance. I don't have it anymore, and I don't know if I could even get it if I wanted to. They sent me a letter threatening to liquidate the shop!"

Sheila gasped. "Patty! How could you hide this from me? All those times I called and asked how you were, you never mentioned *any* of this!"

"It wasn't for you to know," Patty said simply, turning back to face the kitchen counter. The electric tea kettle beeped and she picked it up, pouring the boiling water into the teapot. "I'm only telling you now so you can take care of Derby."

"Patty. That dog adores you." Sheila pointed down at him. He was splayed out on the cool kitchen floor, peering up at Patty. "You can't abandon him in his old age."

"Old age! *I'm* the old one." She shook her head. "I've had a lot of adventures. It's time for this one to end."

"Is that what you want? To leave San Juan Island? To leave your tea shop?"

Patty carried the teapot over and set it on the table. "Neighbors are calling my son to tell him that my home looks abandoned. It's not going to get any better from here. Getting to the store is harder. Getting the laundry down the steps is harder..." She shook her head. "I don't –"

The sound of the front door opening cut her off. A man's voice called out. "Honey?"

Patty's eyes grew as wide as saucers.

"*Honey?*" Sheila repeated in a whisper.

He was getting closer. "Are you home?"

A smile spread across Sheila's face. "Patty, do you have a *boyfriend?*"

Patty sucked in a breath, her cheeks flushing pink. "Of course not. That's the handyman." She raised her voice and yelled out, "I have a guest. You're not needed."

A moment later, the man appeared in the doorway. He was dressed in light blue denim overalls, a green shirt, and a flat cap. He smiled when he saw them sitting there, the wrinkles of his face lighting up when he saw Patty.

"I'm sorry, I'll come back later." He paused. "Wait a minute...you're not Sheila, are you?"

Sheila stood, grinning, and offered a handshake. "I am, sir, and who are you?"

"I'm Reggie."

"The *handyman*," Patty interjected. "There is no need to talk to him."

Sheila turned back to Reggie and raised her eyebrows. "No offense, Reggie, but how handy are you? I heard the house needs a lot of help."

He let out a guffaw and put his hands up. "I'm not here to cause trouble."

"Please, have a seat," Sheila said, motioning to the empty chair next to her. "The tea should be about ready, then you can tell me more about what you've been doing around the cottage."

Despite Patty glaring daggers at him, he sat down and took off his hat. "I've been trying my best, but I can't seem to convince this lady here that we can make it work."

"There's nothing to make work," Patty snapped. "I am moving away."

"No, you're not," Sheila said. "You can't leave. You have a wonderful life here, with your loving dog, and your loving *boyfriend*."

Patty stood. "Oh, stop it! I've outlived two husbands and I'm too old to have a boyfriend!"

Sheila and Reggie laughed.

Patty poured them each a cup of tea, her lips pursed. "I told you, he's the handyman. He's just not very good, which is why the place is falling apart."

"He must have other things on his mind," Sheila said, picking up her teacup and sitting back.

"*Sheila!*" She sat down in a huff. "If you came here to embarrass me –"

Sheila cut her off. "I'm not here to embarrass you! I came here to help you."

"I don't need your help."

Sheila set her cup down and crossed her arms. "Of course you don't. But you aren't acting like yourself at all. You haven't even asked me about getting fired."

Patty took a sip of tea, eyeing her. "I thought you were joking."

Sheila shook her head. "No. I got fired this morning. Right before you called."

She gasped. "How *dare* they fire you! You gave the last ten years to that company –"

"Here's the thing." Sheila leaned in, interrupting her. "The timing couldn't be better. I can see it now! It's a blessing! Really, it is. You needed someone here to give Derby baths and help rename the tea shop and open it again."

"It doesn't need to be renamed," Patty said.

Reggie shrugged. "I think you might want to consider it."

"Listen, my visit can be temporary, but let me help. Let me move in for a bit. I'll pull some weeds, call your insurance, get a painter for the cottage. If you still want to move away in a few months, then fine. At least then I'll know it's on *your* terms."

Patty was quiet for a moment, like she was actually considering it.

Sheila held her breath. She was right. Patty didn't want to leave this place, this home she loved. The boyfriend she'd been hiding.

"I don't know, Sheila."

"Maybe she needs a change, too," Reggie offered. "The sea air can heal hearts, you know."

Sheila's eyes flashed up at him, then back to her teacup. Had Patty told him about her? How bitter she was about Brian and the divorce?

She didn't want to be this way. She didn't want to be bitter and angry and reactive, but that's what she was. It had been five years since the divorce, but Brian could still bait her into reacting so easily. She thought time healed all wounds, but what good was that time when she was merely surviving?

Maybe Reggie was right.

Sheila cleared her throat. "Maybe I do need a change. It's been quiet at home since Emma left for school."

Patty frowned and put a hand on her shoulder. "It's the nights, isn't it? The house feels so empty. So quiet."

The breath was sucked right out of her. Of course Patty knew about how dark and endless the evenings felt.

"Yeah." Sheila sighed. "The nights are...strange."

"What about the girls? What if they expect you to be home, waiting for them?"

"They can come here!" Sheila said, her excitement picking back up. "They love it here. I'll rent our house out, or something." She would need to, just to keep up with the mortgage... "Come on, Patty. If it doesn't work out, then you're no worse off than before."

Patty kept her eyes fixed on her teacup. "I think Brian already has an informal agreement with the neighbor. I'd hate to put them out."

"Your neighbor Barb?" Sheila shrugged. "I'm sure she'd understand if you changed your mind."

"Not her. The *new* neighbor. The actor."

Sheila narrowed her eyes. "Is this about Idris Elba again?"

"No." She leaned in and dropped her voice to whisper, "It's Russell Westwood. He moved into the house next door a few months ago, and he wants to buy my land to make a farm. Or something. I don't know. I didn't want to know."

Sheila could feel the tea burning her throat. Sure, he had been charming enough when she met him on the ferry, but this was too far. Did that hot-shot overly handsome movie star think he could waltz onto the island and take what wasn't his?

She set her cup down. "Russell Westwood, you say? I'm going to pay him a visit."

Seven

The tide report was promising, and Russell didn't want to miss his chance to enjoy the glorious day. He stood on the shore and pulled on a waterproof jacket, the waves gently rocking his kayak in its partially beached position.

He took a step back and sucked in the salty air. He could not get over how beautiful the water was – clear to the bottom, with a blue hue. If it weren't so cold, he would be tempted to jump in for a swim.

He was doing the last of his due diligence and rechecking the weather reports when he heard someone yelling.

The wind filled his ears, so he looked around, searching for the source. It took only a moment to spot her: the woman from the boat, her hair blowing in the wind, the large t-shirt with the howling wolves pulled tight over her small frame.

Here we go, he thought. She'd had some time to think on it, and she decided she wanted something from him.

A picture, if he was lucky. Or she had a script to give him. Or she'd be like that guy who one time asked him for a million dollars.

A *million* dollars!

"Hey there," he said, offering a small wave before turning back to his kayak.

She closed the distance and stood a few feet from him, hands on her hips. "Russell."

He nodded. "You got me."

"Excuse me, I'm talking to you."

He turned to look at her and raised an eyebrow. "Well, I don't mean to be rude, but this is private property and I'm about to get out on the water."

Wouldn't it be funny if he just got in the kayak and paddled away? He could dream...

Her eyes widened. "Is it private property? That's funny, because my mother-in-law's cottage is *also* on private property." She pointed a hand behind her before snapping it back to her hip. "And she is *not* selling. If you think you can come here and take her home away, you've got another thing coming."

The wolves printed on her shirt moved with each rageful point, and he couldn't help it. He cracked a smile.

"Did you not hear what I just said?" she snapped.

"I did, and I'm sorry. I'm not laughing at you. It's – I've never had someone wearing a howling wolf shirt yell at me before."

Her eyes drifted down to her shirt and she frowned. "You're trying to buy the property next door, right? You wanted to start a farm?"

"I had some ideas for the property, yes. I thought it was abandoned."

"Well, it's not. My mother-in-law lives there. Patty. You should get to know her. Be neighborly. Offer to mow her lawn, maybe."

Russell's mouth dropped open. He'd had every intention of being neighborly before moving here. He just didn't know where to start. He knew how not to spook wolves, but not necessarily new neighbors.

"I'm sorry. Believe me, I didn't go looking for trouble. It was your husband who offered to sell it to me in the first place."

"Brian?" She scowled. "He's not my husband."

Come to think of it, he preferred the wolves. If they caught sight of him, they'd run off. There was never any yelling. Never even as much as a growl.

"He offered a good price on it. I thought it was an interesting opportunity. That's all."

"He offered you a good price on it," she repeated, stepping closer. "I bet he did. I bet he told you he was in a hurry to sell."

Russell thought on this for a moment, then nodded. "He did, actually."

She faltered, taking her hands off her hips and letting her arms fall to her sides. "Did he already sell it to you?"

"No. He was going to call to talk about it this week, I think."

"Oh." She crossed her arms. "How much was he asking for it, may I ask?"

All signs pointed to this being a family issue he should steer clear of, but Russell was too amused by this furious little woman to stop talking.

He couldn't remember the last time someone had gone toe-to-toe with him like this. Most of the time, people tried to sweet talk him. Charm him. *I've got a movie you should look at* or *Your fan base would love this. They miss you.*

Her charm was unintentional and wrapped in fury, and it made him feel alive. Engaged. Awake, even.

Russell had to keep the smile off his face, if only to avoid infuriating her more. "He told me he was intending to sell at eight hundred thousand."

She paused, puffing out her cheeks. "I'll admit, I don't know the market around here, but that seems very cheap for ten acres."

"I thought so too," he said with a shrug.

"It's not a done deal." She pointed at him. "Don't talk to Brian anymore."

He opened his mouth to respond as she added a curt "Please."

It was getting extremely difficult not to laugh. Truth be told, he hadn't thought much about the land. It was something offered to him, not something he'd sought out. He wasn't even sure if he could afford it.

But it was best to keep up the façade for her benefit. "Okay. If you say so. I won't talk to him anymore."

She spun a black purse to her hip, digging inside, and pulled out a business card. "If he contacts you again, I want you to tell me. Call the cell, not the, uh, other number."

Sheila Dennet, Accountant. "You're a numbers person, eh?"

"That's right," she said, and before he could ask anything else, she spoke again. "I'm going to call Brian right now and clear this up. Have fun on your kayak."

With that, she spun around and stormed back up the hill.

Russell stood there, watching as she grew smaller and smaller. A laugh escaped from him, and he scratched the back of his head and looked around.

Had anyone else witnessed that?

It seemed not. The beach was deserted, and apart from a few seagulls, he was alone.

Life could still surprise him, apparently.

He stooped down to pick up his paddle and saw a newspaper clipping clinging to the rocks.

He picked it up, shaking the few drops of water it had managed to absorb, and called out. "Sheila! You dropped something!"

She was too far gone, and the wind carried his voice over the sea. He unpeeled a stuck corner, the headline catching his eye.

BELOVED KILLER WHALE DIES BEFORE CHANCE TO RETURN HOME
August 19th, 2023

Only months after her release back to the ocean was announced, Tokitae, also known as Lolita or Sk'aliCh'elh-tenaut, died yesterday in Miami. She was 57 years old.

Believed to be four when captured off the coast of Washington State in 1970, Tokitae was known for her gentle nature and lively spirit. During her capture, four baby whales drowned while trying to reach their mothers, and whale hunts were banned soon after.

The decades of captures had a lasting effect on Washington's Southern Resident whales, known as J, K, and L pods. It's believed approximately 40% of the population was captured or killed, and the population remains critically endangered to this day.

Tokitae was the last living captive member of the Southern Resident whales, and her death comes as a shock to many. Animal welfare activists and the Lummi tribe have fought for years for her release from captivity. In recent years, there were plans to retire Tokitae to her native waters to live the rest of her years in a sea pen.

Orcas are social animals, and despite not living with other orcas in decades, Tokitae still called out in her native dialect. There were hopes of a reunion between her and her mother, L-25 Ocean Sun, the oldest-living Southern Resident whale.

An autopsy will be completed to investigate her cause of death.

Eight

Pushing away the vague feeling she was acting rashly, Sheila pulled out her phone and called Brian. She was halfway back to the cottage when it dawned on her that she hadn't heard Brian's voice in over a year.

She slowed her pace. Normally, they did all their communicating through email. Sheila's lawyer had suggested it years ago, and it worked well enough. Communicating with him was an area where she'd had to build grace.

His emails were so cold, so measured. It felt like she was talking to a stranger, not her husband of twenty-two years. Her favorite email was from before their divorce was finalized. The subject was "FYI," and the content was, "I will be moving to New York in six weeks. My attorney will be contacting you about our parenting plan."

That email had *really* tested her grace.

This moment was a new test, and she didn't have time to find a way to do it gracefully.

The ringing stopped and cut to his voicemail.

Maybe if he didn't want to answer his phone, she could email him using his own style? Subject, "By the way," content, "Your mom isn't moving."

No. That was unwise, and she was being petty. She had gone so long without letting him get to her, but here she was, glaring out at the ocean and letting little malevolent thoughts wash over her.

She paused and let out a sigh. She knew what he was going to say. Tell her it wasn't her business. Tell her to stay out of it.

How could she, though, when she had seen the sadness in Patty's eyes? When she'd met Patty's secret boyfriend whom she refused to admit was her boyfriend?

Sheila took a seat on a bench facing the water. She'd been through enough therapy to know that what she was doing was unproductive, but she couldn't stop herself.

She called him again, and this time, the call went to voicemail much sooner.

He must have declined the call.

The nerve.

She shot up from the bench and stomped back to the cottage, pushed open the door, and blew into the kitchen. Patty and Reggie were still sitting there, and they turned in surprise when she burst in.

"Everything all right?" Patty asked wearily.

"You don't have to worry about Russell Westwood," Sheila said. "I think I've scared him off."

"Sheila. I didn't ask you to do that."

She tossed her purse onto the kitchen counter. "You didn't have to."

"I've been thinking," Patty said, slowly standing from her seat. "You're at a delicate time in your life."

Sheila's eyes flitted up to her momentarily before redialing Brian's number.

Three calls. He had to answer. What if she was calling about an emergency? Shouldn't he have the decency to answer at least once? "I don't need you to tell me I'm old."

"You're not old. You're middle-aged," Patty said matter-of-factly, as if that would make her feel any better. "It's still a delicate time. A transition. You're used to being so many things to so many people. Maybe it's time for you to think about yourself."

Sheila got his voicemail again and hung up. "I don't even know what that means."

"Exactly," Patty said gently, holding her hands up as though trying to defuse a bomb. "Maybe if you –"

"You're not going to convince me to leave, Patty. There is nowhere else in the world I'd rather be than here, with you, in this cottage."

That was easy for her to say it so forcefully because it was, in fact, the truth. And because there were a lot of things she didn't want to face right now.

Sheila knew she was middle-aged. She knew she had an empty nest. She also knew she was broke and she'd just gotten fired.

To her horror, she'd become a statistic. A woman teetering on the edge of bankruptcy after a divorce.

No one *wants* to become a statistic; it just happens. While Brian excitedly planned the new life he'd dreamt up, complete with Christmas cards of his new family in matching pajamas,

Sheila was out there doing the stuff no one took pictures of: scrubbing the slime off the shower. Running a bake sale for the third time that year. Getting mascara out of the bathroom towels for the hundredth time because her teenage daughter hadn't been asked to prom.

Yet, all the while, she knew Brian had it wrong. On the eve of finalizing their divorce, he'd left her a message.

"You're nothing without me," he'd said, the disgust curled in his voice.

Every moment since then, she'd proven him wrong. She wasn't going to stop now.

"I don't want to go back home. I'm going to rent out the house while I'm here," Sheila said out loud. "I think that would be smart."

Patty and Reggie looked at each other, then back at her.

"Are you sure you're okay, Sheila?" Patty asked. "You seem to be repeating yourself."

"Yes." She held out her hand, palm up. "Let me see your phone."

Without questioning it, Patty walked over to the kitchen counter, picked up her phone, and handed it to Sheila. "Why do you need my phone?"

"I've heard about this," Reggie said. "It's a scam against the elderly. This must be how it starts."

Sheila laughed out loud. "No. It's just that Brian won't answer when I call."

Patty frowned but said nothing.

Sheila dialed him again, and this time, he picked up after two rings. "Hey, Mom. Everything okay?"

He sounded the same, the same tenor to his voice, the same clearing of the throat. This stranger who had her husband's voice.

"Hello, Brian." Sheila smiled. "I've been trying to reach you."

"Is Mom okay?"

Sheila opened the back door and slipped outside. "She's fine, except for you trying to sell her home."

"Here we go."

Sheila dropped her voice. "Do you really think your mother is going to survive a move across the country to a place she's never been?"

"Spare me. I'm doing what's best for her."

Sheila knew she shouldn't say it, but she couldn't help herself. All the pressure from the day forced her into a strange place where everything that passed between them felt like it had just happened moments—not years—ago. "What's best for her, or what's best for you?"

"Sheila. I don't have time for this."

Like he didn't have time to see his daughter off to college? Or make the trip for soccer games, or birthdays, or the day Shelby got her braces off and they all went to get ice cream?

Her kids deserved better, and so did Patty.

"That's fine," Sheila said, her voice steady. "I just wanted to let yould know she's not interested in selling the property anymore."

"Oh great. Instead, she can fall again with no one to find her and –"

Sheila cut him off. "I'm going to be here with her. I'm going to help her get back on her feet and open the tea shop."

He scoffed. "What is this, *Grey Gardens*? Are you finally getting to live out your fantasy?"

Sheila let out a huff of air. It was so like him to jab her with something she loved. She'd always been fascinated by the *Grey Gardens* documentary – the two aging, genteel women in their dilapidated mansion, raccoons running in and out of the attic, cats on every surface.

It was a story of a mother and a daughter, tragic and fascinating and *human*, so of course Brian would miss the point entirely. "This is nothing like *Grey Gardens*."

"That's right, because she's not your actual mother. Where is your mother, by the way? Shouldn't you be tracking her down? Finding out if she's even alive?"

The sun's rays were powerful enough to warm her skin, but not warm enough to stop the chill running through her veins.

Bringing her mother into this was a low blow, but she shouldn't have expected anything else from him. Her mom had been in and out of her life for years, starting from the time she was nine years old. Sheila had learned to live without her, even thrive without her.

But then she'd met Patty. Patty was like the mother she'd never had, and there was no way she would take her for granted the way Brian did.

That was enough talking to him for the year. "Don't worry about my mother. Just know your mom isn't selling. Good-bye."

She made sure the call was ended before she screamed into the wind.

Then she took a deep breath and smoothed her hair.

It hadn't been their most polite conversation, but it had been productive. Yes, she'd gotten a bit worked up, but she wasn't ashamed. She felt invigorated.

She was tired of holding herself back, holding her tongue, holding it together. Something broke five years ago, and it wasn't just her marriage.

It felt like she'd been running on a treadmill since the divorce, constantly picking up speed, without a moment to just *breathe*. She was busy making sure the girls were okay, busy trying to keep the house from falling into foreclosure, busy working to keep them afloat...

She'd put all her effort into trying to survive, and now she was here, with the sun on her face and sea air in her lungs, and something just *snapped.*

Patty was right. She was in a delicate state. Fired from her job, about to lose her home, and a burglary box burning a hole in her trunk on the mainland.

She'd made it, though. She was alive, and she was here, with an expanse of possibilities ahead. It was terrifying and thrilling, a mix she hadn't felt for too long.

Sheila ran a hand through her hair and drew her shoulders straight. She wasn't going to be held down anymore.

Nine

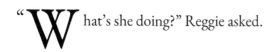

"What's she doing?" Reggie asked.

Patty peered out of the kitchen window. "I don't know. She's not on the phone anymore. She's just standing there."

"Should I go and get her?"

"No!" Patty spun around. "You shouldn't be here at all. Now she knows about you."

Reggie chuckled. "She was bound to find out sooner or later."

"Not if I hadn't called her." Patty shot him a glance, and he said nothing, looking up at her with mischief in his eyes.

He was too adorable to stay angry with. She took a seat next to him. "You're right, and I knew exactly how this would go. I knew she'd come up here and insist on saving me."

"There's nothing wrong with wanting to be saved every now and then." Reggie patted her on the leg and planted a kiss on her cheek. "I'll get going, but I'll be back tonight with a pot roast and some mashed potatoes."

It was nice being saved every once in a while, and Reggie liked to save her every chance he got. "I just wish it hadn't started a fight between them. Between Brian and Sheila."

Reggie shrugged. "That wasn't your doing. They're going to fight anyway."

She sighed. "I know."

He stood and planted another kiss on her before walking to the front door.

Patty sat there, combing through her thoughts. Brian had lost his way. She didn't know if it was a midlife crisis or just him running away from his problems. She'd tried talking to him about it a dozen times, but he'd dismissed her. He shut down.

He was fifty years old but acting the same way he had when he was a teenager. All that was missing was for him to run up the stairs and slam the door on her.

Maybe she should've pushed him more then? Insisted he talk out his feelings? It had started after his dad died – Patty's first husband.

She thought Brian would come around in his own time, but he never outgrew it. He still ran off and refused to talk to anyone about how he felt or what he was thinking.

The back door opened and Sheila appeared. Her hair looked a bit wild from the wind, but her expression was serene. Without a word, she closed the door, returned Patty's phone to the counter, and took a seat.

"Did you argue?" Patty asked.

"We disagreed," Sheila said. "But that's okay. We don't have to agree on everything."

"I'm afraid I'm putting too much on you." Patty wrung her hands together. "I don't want to come between you and Brian. Whatever peace you've cobbled together –"

Sheila held up a hand. "Patty, please. We've got bigger things to worry about. Like what we're going to rename the tea shop."

A smile spread across her face and Patty laughed. She couldn't help it. It was foolish of her to think she could stop Sheila. The woman had never been stopped in her life. "I'm betting you already have a name picked out."

"I've got some ideas."

"You know, I'd love to hire you full-time, but I'm not making any money."

"Don't worry about money. My wheels are already turning," Sheila said. "Maybe one of the girls can help us set up a website. Eliza? She's always up for a challenge. We'll get a new name, a new website, and a new vibe, as the kids say."

"A new 'vibe'!" Patty laughed. "Listen to you."

"I think I can pick up some accounting clients on the island, too. It's full of rich people, right?"

Patty chuckled. "It does feel that way sometimes." She paused. "Did they give a reason for firing you? What happened?"

Sheila frowned. "It's a long story. I don't think I'm ready to tell you yet."

"But you will? Tell me?"

"Of course. Right after I make up my mind about what I'm going to do."

"Maybe I could help you make up your mind? Keep you from doing anything...reckless?"

Sheila laughed. "Says the woman who decided to become a beekeeper after finding a queen bee once."

"That was the right decision at the time," Patty said, standing up to search for cookies to go with their tea. "I only hope you can be so wise."

Ten

The kayak trip offered views of rocky bluffs, glimpses of round-bodied harbor seals, and flashes of bald eagles flying above, yet the entire time, all Russell could see was Sheila. In his mind's eye, she was still glaring at him, her face twisted in a furious scowl, her finger wildly pointing over the trees.

She was right, of course. About everything. His intention in moving to the island was to learn to live amongst people again. Learn to trust, learn to make friends – learn to *be* a friend again.

There weren't any lasting friendships in Los Angeles, and when Holly had decided she was sick of Hollywood and wanted to move back to Minneapolis, he was thrilled.

His fame faded and they raised the kids in suburban bliss. They had loads of friends there, but in recent years, those relationships had started to run cold.

It had all started when Holly begged him to do "one last movie." His resurging fame seeped in and poisoned the goodwill he'd had with so many neighbors and acquaintances. Even the principal of his kids' school approached him with an idea for a rap album.

He had to put walls up to keep people out – not just for his own sanity, but for the sake of his kids. For a while, at least, they still had some wonderful friends.

But even those started to recede after the divorce. Through some secret process, people picked sides. It wasn't done as part of the official divorce mediation. It was done in the silence, the absence of phone calls, the missing invites to the annual Labor Day cookout.

It wasn't all of Russell's friends, but it was enough. Enough to make him feel alone, enough to make him want to run. And so, after the kids went off to college, he left.

Even that was short-lived, though. He realized he couldn't bury himself in the snow and watch wolves forever. There was a lot of life left to live. The wolves didn't thrive alone, and neither could he.

The next morning, Russell made up his mind to do better. He was going to be neighborly if it killed him – likely from Sheila's glare – and he'd do it the only way he knew how: in excess.

He woke early, drove to the bakery in town, and picked up a few things – little sour cream coffee cakes, scones, croissants, and a raspberry oat butter tart. He split the baked peace offerings into four boxes, enough to meet all his nearest neighbors, and headed to his first stop: Sheila's mother-in-law's house.

He drove up the driveway slowly, admiring the trees, the grasses, and the silhouette of the cottage against the sea. Even when Brian had offered to sell the property to him, he hadn't spent much time *really* looking at it. It was beautiful and had a peaceful ease his own home lacked. It was as though the cottage belonged with the ocean, as though it had always been there.

He walked up to the front door and knocked. A moment later, an older woman answered.

She smiled, looking him up and down. "Are you selling Boy Scout cookies? Because I am not interested!"

Russell sucked in a breath, still holding the bakery box in front of him like a dope. "Er, no, I'm –"

The woman laughed and patted him on the shoulder. "I'm only pretending I don't know who you are. Of course I know you!"

The sudden break in the tension caused him to laugh. "Russell Westwood," he said. "It's a pleasure to meet you. I wanted to apologize for not introducing myself earlier."

"You have nothing to apologize for." She stepped to the side and waved a hand. "I'm Patty Dennet. Please, come on in!"

He stepped inside, breathing in the smell of cinnamon and coffee. A wonderful mix. "These are for you...from the bakery. I won't pretend to have made them myself."

"Well, Russell, it seems we're about to do a sweets exchange." She accepted the box, smiling as she peeked inside. "I just pulled some of my world-famous cinnamon rolls out of the oven. Would you like one?"

He nodded. "Yes, please."

She led him down the hall and into a small kitchen. "Coffee? Tea?" she asked, opening a cupboard.

"I'm all right. I don't mean to trouble you."

"We're neighbors! It's no trouble. People used to pop over all the time. That's changed now, you know? People don't just come over anymore." She pointed at the table in the corner. "Sit down! Please."

Russell took a seat at the kitchen table. "Yes, things have changed."

"You can feel free to stop by anytime," Patty continued. "I used to have a little tea shop I ran, too, but..." She tapped her chin. "That's a topic for another day."

"Who are you talking to?" called out a voice. "If you're talking to yourself, then I'll be forced to make a video for the doctor."

Sheila appeared in the doorway, and when her eyes fell on him, she froze.

He stood to shake her hand. "Hi, Sheila. It's nice to see you again."

She wasn't dressed as a wolf super-fan anymore. Instead, she had on a pair of dark jeans, a hole at the knee, and a washed-out t-shirt with a monkey on it.

He tilted his head to the side. "Your shirt – is that from the Pixies?"

She nodded. "I'm a fan. Or used to be. I thought I'd lost this shirt for good."

"Turns out I'd stolen it!" Patty cackled a laugh as she poured hot water into a teapot. "I guess I took some clothes to wash last time you were visiting and, well, there you go. You should've come sooner."

Russell reached into his pocket and pulled out his wallet. "I think I have something of yours, too."

Sheila eyed him. "Oh?"

"You dropped it yesterday." He delicately removed the newspaper clipping he'd picked off the beach. "Is this yours?"

Her eyes darted down and she accepted it with a delicate hand. "Yeah, thank you."

He didn't know how to ask her what it was about, though he was keen to know why she'd carried it with her.

Luckily, Patty had no hesitations. "What's that?"

"Just a news story from my birthday."

Patty plopped a plate on the table with a large, gooey cinnamon roll. "If you don't want coffee or tea, I have milk, too."

"That's all right," he laughed. "Coffee would be perfect."

In a flash, a mug appeared next to his plate. Patty set a french press next to it. "Cream?"

"Yes please."

She darted off to the fridge, and he looked up to see Sheila still eyeing him.

Patty bumped her with her hip. "Sit down. I have one for you too."

"I'm not hungry, and I need to catch the ferry anyway."

"You have time for a cinnamon roll. Now *sit!*"

Patty pointed and Sheila listened to her, sliding into a chair. "Where's Derby?"

"He's outside on his tie-out. He's really started to enjoy looking at the ocean in his old age," Patty said. "Starting to appreciate the finer things, I guess."

Russell took his first bite of the still-warm cinnamon roll. As good as everything he'd gotten from the bakery looked, it couldn't beat this. "This is delicious. Thank you."

"You're welcome!" Patty had her back turned, unloading the bakery box he'd brought onto a plate.

Sheila watched her with a half-smile on her face.

"Do you like the bakery in town?" he asked.

She turned sharply, as if she'd forgotten he was there. "Oh. Yes."

She seemed to be somewhere else entirely. Sort of how she'd looked when he first saw her on the ferry. "I actually had something to ask you."

Sheila poured herself a cup of tea. "Hm?"

"The card you gave me, it said you're an accountant. Is that right?"

"Why?"

Being neighborly was much harder than he'd expected. "I was hoping to...I was actually looking for an accountant."

She set her teacup down. "I don't think that's a good idea. I'm not with that firm anymore."

Patty appeared, this time with an empty teacup for herself. "Why not? You were just telling me you needed clients."

She gave a non-committal shrug, her eyes darting to Russell, then back to her teacup.

"You don't have to answer now," Russell said. "I understand if you're busy."

"She's not too busy. We're neighbors!" Patty sat down, a grin on her face. "Right, Sheila? She'll be coming to stay with me for a bit."

"Yeah." Sheila took a cinnamon roll and put it onto a plate. "I'll be here so...I suppose I could take a look."

"Thank you. I appreciate it," he said, stuffing his mouth with another bite of the warm cinnamon bun.

As mysterious as Sheila was, there was also something familiar about her. It could be something in those deep brown eyes and how when she stared, lost in thought, her dark hair slowly falling in front of her face.

He had to resist the urge to tuck the hair behind her ear. It was startling that the thought even occurred to him. How bizarre would it be to reach out and touch someone who was not only a stranger, but one who didn't like him particularly much?

She reminded him of someone who didn't want to be followed, someone who didn't want to be tracked. He would stay back. Watch from afar. He was good at that.

If he was quiet enough, perhaps she'd let down her guard and let him into that mind of hers.

Eleven

The kitchen was too warm. Sheila sank into her chair, clutching her teacup with both hands and stealing glances at Russell as he talked and joked with Patty.

In the sober morning light, it was much harder for her to remember why she had felt so justified in yelling at Russell Westwood.

Not only did she not know the man, but he was *famous!* She might as well have been yelling at George Clooney or Matt Damon. Russell's charm and handsomeness was not gone just because he'd grown a beard!

Who did she think she was, acting like that? Russell had been perfectly reasonable and polite. She had behaved like a mad woman.

Sheila cleared her throat and pushed away the cinnamon bun Patty had forced on her. The sweet smell reminded her too much of the hot chocolate, and the donuts, and the presentation.

It was a frenzy. That was what had happened to her. Ever since she'd gotten up at three in the morning to prepare those donuts, she'd been in a frenzy. It carried her through a traumatic firing, a fight she'd started with Brian, and threatening an A-list actor.

Here she was, back on earth where she belonged, avoiding eye contact with him, yet unable to stop staring.

"Speaking of your birthday," Patty said, "we never got to celebrate last month. I'm going to make that lemon blueberry cake you like."

Russell's gaze turned to her, but Sheila kept her eyes fixed on Patty. "No, that's okay."

"Come on! You never want to celebrate your birthday."

"There's nothing to celebrate." People put too much hope into birthdays. Sheila would be much happier if everyone forgot hers existed. "I really have to get going, Patty."

Patty sighed and wiped her hands on her apron. "Oh, all right, all right. Go ahead and rush the only celebrity that I've ever met out of my house and run him onto the –"

Russell laughed. "I'll come back. You don't have to worry about that. If I smell cinnamon, I'll be back."

Patty's face lit up with a smile. "That would be *lovely*. Any time. I mean it!" She clapped her hands together. "Actually, I once met Paul Newman on Daytona Beach. I pointed at him and said, 'That's Paul Newman!' and he pointed back and said, 'Keep my secret!'" She touched a hand to her chest. "Listen to me babbling on like an old woman. But, just so you know, you're not the only celebrity I've ever met."

"I don't hold a candle to Paul Newman," Russell said, shaking his head.

Patty chuckled. "I wouldn't go that far. You're very good, you know that?"

Russell smiled. "You're kind, but I'm your neighbor now. Don't be afraid to ask for help if you ever need it."

Patty clasped her hands together as though she'd just been struck with an idea. "I do have weeds you can pull out front! And trim the lavender, while you're at it. So much of it has withered and died."

"No problem," he said with a nod. "I'll get right on that."

"I'm kidding, I'm kidding!" Patty laughed and tapped him on the shoulder. "It is nice to have you, though. The last owner of your house was hardly ever here. It was a vacation home, and a neglected one, I suspect."

"It was in need of an update. I'd love to show you sometime." He stood and carried his dishes to the sink. "Can I at least wash these dishes?"

Sheila suppressed a laugh. It didn't matter how fast Russell was; he'd never get near that sponge.

"No!" Patty yanked the dishes from him. "You're my guest!"

Sheila stared, holding her breath. Would he try to wrestle the plates back from her? Patty had a deceptively strong grip, probably from years of playing tug-of-war with Derby.

He seemed to sense this and let it go. "Thank you for being so welcoming today. I'm sorry about the misunderstanding with your son. I'm not trying to steal your home from you. I promise I won't cause any more trouble."

Shoot. There it was. He'd beaten her to it. Sheila was going to bring up their confrontation and be the one to apologize.

Instead, she'd sat there like a mute.

It looked like Patty was about to reach out and pinch his cheek, but thankfully, she resisted. "Water under the bridge."

"Maybe we can talk business soon, Sheila?" he asked.

She nodded and cleared her throat. "Yes. Sure."

Patty took him by the arm and walked him to the front door.

When she returned, she stood with her hands on her hips. "Would you look at that? You hear about these Hollywood types being awful, but he really was lovely."

"Maybe he was acting," Sheila said with a half-smile.

She cleared her plate and walked down the hallway. Patty followed.

"He's *very* handsome in person," Patty went on. "Maybe not as good-looking as your Idris Elba, but you have to admit, he's handsome."

Sheila picked up her purse. "Why do you keep bringing up Idris Elba? I think you have a crush on him, not me."

"Don't be ridiculous! He's much too young for me. He's your age, I think. *Fifty!*" She scoffed and opened the door. "Fifty is a great age, though. You're going to love it."

Except it wasn't going that well so far. Sheila wouldn't get her hopes up. "We'll see. I'm going to go home and sort out a few things with the house, but I'll be back soon. I'll talk to Eliza about the website. I think she can help, and I'll get right to work."

Patty nodded. "I believe you. Who knows? Maybe Russell can help us too."

She winked and Sheila decided to ignore that entirely. "Can I get a ride to the ferry now? Please? Or am I going to have to hitchhike?"

"All right! You can't rush someone of my vintage. I'm going." She led the way to the car and once they were on the road, she spoke again. "Why do you hate your birthday so much? Is it because of your mom?"

She kept her eyes on the window, watching the trees as they passed. When she was newly married, Patty never mentioned Sheila's mom. It took years for Patty to even whisper her name, worried it would upset her.

Sheila was, thankfully, beyond that. Her mother's absence in her childhood used to smolder inside of her like a tree struck by lightning. Anything could spark a flame.

But once she had her own children, once she saw how easy it was for her to *not* repeat her mother's mistakes, her perspective changed. She saw her mother as the lost child she was, a woman who swooped in occasionally to relay the new injustices she'd suffered and to complain about her grandkids' loud voices hurting her ears.

"Not exactly," Sheila said. "She didn't leave on my birthday. It was two weeks before."

"Oh." Patty was quiet, then added, "We still have birthdays to make up for, then. I'm going to make you that cake. Maybe I'll make two."

Sheila smiled. "Just as long as you don't try to invite your crush over."

"Reggie?" Patty asked. "Cat's out of the bag on that one."

"Not him. I meant Idris Elba."

They both erupted into laughter, and Sheila was glad her joke did the trick. She didn't want to talk about that birthday anymore. There was no point.

She *did* have a cake that year, though. Her dad had made it himself. Chocolate, dry and burnt at the edges, smothered in store-bought chocolate. She'd loved it.

He had to do so much after their mom left. He wasn't perfect, but he tried. There was no resentment in her anymore. She could feel in her bones how much he'd loved them all, how he did what he thought was right...

Sheila looked through the window, trying to think of something else. Anything else. She didn't want her mind to drift back to that day. She'd gotten so good at not thinking about it, not even remembering it was real.

Until recently. Maybe that was when the frenzy had really started.

Once she was on the ferry back to the mainland, alone with her thoughts, Sheila was too tired to avoid it any longer. She let the memory wash over her, like the tide in the moonlight, pulling her into the darkness.

August 8th, 1982

S heila's mom left them that day. It was a week and a half before Sheila's ninth birthday.

Sheila was the eldest, and she fully embraced her role as the new primary caregiver of her sisters. "Mom is just visiting her great aunt," she confidently told her two younger sisters. "She'll be back soon."

It was a lie, of course, but one she wanted to believe. There was no great aunt. Sheila had read about a needy aunt in a book at school, and it seemed as possible as anything else.

Her dad offered no explanations because he had none. He sent them to his sister's house while he worked, riding out on his fishing boat every morning, and relied on precocious Sheila to fill in the gaps.

She was proud to help. It felt like her duty, as well as tending to the cleaning and getting her sisters ready for bed every night.

Every day, she found something new to do, something that would cheer her mother when she finally came home. She scrubbed the bathroom, organized the messy kitchen cabinets, pulled the weeds from the garden, and baked batch after batch of brownies.

After a week, her mom still hadn't returned to sample the brownies and Sheila started to panic. Her dad found her on the front porch late that night, pacing back and forth.

"What's the matter, Sheil?" he asked, though he knew full well what caused his daughter's distress.

She finally worked up the courage to say it out loud. "When is she coming back, Dad?"

The look on his face told her everything she needed to know. His eyes were rimmed with tears, his face scruffy and wrinkled. "I don't know, Sheil."

Secretly, she was sure her mom would be back for her birthday, with stories to tell, hugs to give, her arms full of presents.

On the morning of her birthday, Sheila put on her best dress, tidied the house, and waited.

She was allowed to stay home while her sisters went to their friends' houses.

She waited, and waited, and waited.

Her dad came home from work early. "I have something to show you," he said.

He took off through the back door, weaving along the trails in the forest behind their house.

Sheila was hardly able to keep up with his long strides. "Where are we going?"

"I've got something for you," he said, looking over his shoulder. "I caught it yesterday."

He'd had plenty of interesting catches through the years – fish with pretty-colored scales, lost hats, and even a life-sized plastic Santa once.

"Is Mom going to be there?" she asked, but he didn't answer, instead pressing on.

They were almost to the water when she heard it – an awful, wailing cry, repeating over and over.

Her dad reached the shore first, and when she caught up, she put her hands on her knees to catch her breath.

That was when she saw it – a black fin towering over the water.

"Dad!" she gasped. "Is that a whale?"

As if she'd heard, the orca bobbed her head from the water, spy hopping for a moment before dropping back beneath the surface.

"Happy birthday, Sheila!" Her dad said, beaming. "The little one got caught in my net yesterday. I was able to get her out before she drowned. She's a sweet little thing. Feisty. Reminded me of you."

Sheila stumbled forward, tripping and falling into the rocks sloping down to the water. She picked her head up as the smaller whale, closer to them, swam over.

Sheila could not take her eyes off the little orca, who, also curious, was now peering at her from the water. She had a black freckle on her white chin, and her fin was tiny compared to her mother's.

She laid on her side, looking at them. Sheila was close enough to look her in the eye.

"That's a baby?"

"About four or five." He grinned at her. "What do you think?"

"She's beautiful." Sheila watched as the little whale blew out a breath, then swam back toward the net separating her from her mother.

"I was thinking we could get McDonald's tonight. Whatever you want," her dad said.

The baby whale swam along the length of the net, her mother crying out on the other side.

"She's sad, Dad. You have to let her out of there."

He took a deep breath. "I will. Soon. What do you think? Burgers?"

The cries carried over the water, louder now.

It was the most gut-wrenching sound Sheila had ever heard. "Please, Dad. She needs to go back to her mom."

He put a hand on her shoulder and tried to steer her away. "Ice cream, too?"

She wiggled away. "It's not my birthday until Mom comes home."

"Don't act like that," he said. "Not today. Cut me some slack, Sheila."

"It's not my birthday!" she screamed, stomping her foot.

His smile faded and he let out a sigh. Without a word, he turned and walked back into the trees.

For the first time since her mother left, Sheila cried. Her sobs rang out in waves, racking her little body until she was dizzy.

She sat down at the water's edge, and when she looked up, the little whale was there again, watching her.

"I'm sorry," she said.

Sheila sat there until it grew dark, then returned as soon as the sun rose the next morning, then the next, and the next. She named the little whale Lottie after Charlotte Caffey from The Go-Go's and did what she could to help her – singing to her, frantically trying to undo her father's net. It proved impossible for her little hands.

"I *promise* I'll get you back to your mom," she whispered on what would be their last evening together.

Her father refused to talk to her about Lottie, ignoring her pleas, even when the man with the crane showed up. Even as he loaded Lottie into his truck, even as he drove away.

Her dad told her they needed the money. He told her Lottie would be taken care of. He said it was final and he would never talk about it again.

Sheila's mother came back a month later, but it was too late. Too late for Sheila's birthday, too late to save Lottie. Too late for everything.

Her mom stayed for the weekend, then told them she had to go. It would be another six months before she stopped by again.

Sheila never told her about Lottie. She never told *anyone* about her, or the promise she'd made – and failed to keep.

• • •

After her father passed away, Sheila was the only one left with that memory. Until a few months ago, she'd assumed Lottie was dead.

In a twist of fate, she was brought in as the lead accountant for a local theme park, Marine Magic Funland. It was there she got to know the accounts person, the janitor, the security guards, and even the whale trainers. It was there she saw a lone orca in a small tank, with a small black freckle on her chin.

"You're not going to believe it," the trainer said, beaming, "but Lottie's the sweetest whale I've ever met."

In that moment, it all hit her, square in the chest. The way a mother whale's cry carried over the water, the way the saltwater stung the cuts on her hands from digging at the ropes on the net.

Maybe it was the seed for her frenzy. That moment, looking back at the whale trainer. "I believe you," Sheila had said, gripping a hand on the edge of the tank. "I do."

Twelve

S elling their furniture to internet strangers wasn't Eliza's
idea of a good time, but it had to be done.

"Oh! There. A black truck just pulled up." Her roommate
Cora turned from the window. "Did he tell you what kind of
car he'd be driving?"

Eliza shook her head. "I forgot to ask."

It wasn't an area she was experienced in. It was borne from
necessity: Cora's shopping problem. Her best friend was a dear
and lovely person, but she just couldn't get this vice under
control.

She'd finally admitted to Eliza she'd been taking their rent
and "reallocating" it for the past few months.

"How bad is it this time, Cora?" Eliza had asked.

"I'm four thousand in debt." Cora hung her head low. "My
parents say they won't bail me out this time. Please don't hate
me, but we're going to be evicted at the end of the month."

They'd been best friends since they were in high school.
Eliza was angry with her, furious even, but more than that, she
was worried. Cora seemed to be getting deeper in debt with
every passing month, and there was no end in sight. She'd
grown up with money – tons of it – and she was not adjusting
well to her parents finally cutting her off.

"They're coming up the sidewalk!" Cora yelled out. "What do we do? Should I bark so he thinks we have a big dog?"

Normally she would've encouraged Cora to do something as ridiculous as barking, but their current circumstances didn't put her in the most jovial mood. "I'll answer the door. It's fine."

"What if he tries to rob us?"

Eliza paused as she reached the front door of the apartment. "Rob us of what? We don't have anything."

Cora frowned. "That's true."

Eliza opened the door just as Cora added, "What if he tries to kill us?"

There were two men standing there in nearly matching jeans and flannel shirts. The one nearer to the door laughed. "We were worried you might try to kill us, too."

Eliza took a deep breath and forced a smile. "We won't if you won't."

"Deal."

"I was hoping to get the couch outside for you," Eliza turned, pointing behind her. "But we haven't gotten to it yet."

"That's all right. We can carry it."

She stepped aside and he walked in with his friend. They circled around the old leather couch for twenty seconds.

"Five hundred, right?" he said, reaching into his pocket.

Eliza nodded. "That's right."

The friend spoke up. "I don't know, man. This couch looks a little slumpy in the middle. You shouldn't pay more than four. Maybe three-fifty."

Cora stalked over, her hands on her hips. "Five hundred or we walk!"

Eliza shot her a look. Not only was she the reason they had to sell their stuff in a hurry, now she was going to play hardball and negotiate?

He held out his hand. "Ignore him. Five hundred is fine."

She accepted the money, then watched as they stooped and carried the couch out the front door and onto the bed of the truck.

"Whew! That was easy. Nothing to worry about at all," Cora said brightly, shutting the door behind them and locking it.

Eliza stared at her. She had to resist making any comments. She knew this wasn't easy for her, despite her cheer. "Here. Half to you, half to me."

"Thanks." She looked down at the money and made a face. "Are you always going to be mad at me?"

Eliza sighed. "I'm done being mad at you, Cora. You just need to...you need to take care of yourself. Get better."

"Because you can't be angrier at me than *I* am at me," Cora continued, taking a seat on the carpet where the couch had once been. "I have to move back in with my parents because of this stupid shopping problem. Do you know what that's like?"

"Funnily enough, I do." Eliza crossed her arms. "I have to move back in with my mom, too."

Cora waved a hand. "I *wish* I could move in with your mom. Your mom's so cool."

That was true. Her mom was the best.

At the same time, her mom never would have let Cora steal the rent for all those months. She was far too responsible and far too careful with money to let something like that happen.

Eliza found it hard to believe that her parents had met playing in a band. Her mother wasn't *that* kind of cool. She didn't party. She never broke the rules and she never made mistakes.

"Yeah," Eliza said, walking back to her room. "She's the best."

"Does she ever yell at you?" Cora asked, following. "What about when you dropped out of school?"

Eliza shook her head. "No. It's not really her style."

"I guess that's why you don't yell at me. Honestly, it'd make me feel better if you did."

She stopped and smiled. "I'm not going to yell at you. Just get better, okay?"

"I will. I *am* getting better!"

Eliza walked into her bedroom and picked up a box from the floor. Cora grabbed the remaining box and followed her outside. They loaded everything into Eliza's car without a word.

Eliza turned to the driver's door and Cora pulled her in for a long hug. "I'm going to miss you."

She hugged her back. "I'm going to miss you, too. You jerk."

Cora laughed and pulled away, tears in her eyes. "Thanks for that. Okay, bye. Be good."

Eliza waved her off and got into the driver's seat. "*You* be good!"

. . .

She'd decided to surprise her mom about moving back home. It made it feel more like a spontaneous idea and less like the sad situation it was.

She felt sad for Cora. She felt sad for herself, working in a dead-end job at a candle store, unable to come up with the back rent to keep their adorable apartment.

No one would guess by looking at her, but she'd once been considered a prodigy. She'd skipped a grade in school and placed nationally in chess competitions. She was deemed gifted in math and had taken college math classes from the time she was fourteen. The University of Chicago had offered her a full scholarship, and she took it, so sure she was going places.

And then what? She dropped out junior year and hadn't been able to find her way through life since. It felt like the only thing she was good at was failure.

Now she was moving back home at the age of twenty-four. Some prodigy she'd turned out to be.

When she pulled up to the house, she was surprised to see her mom in the driveway, fussing with a pink box in the trunk of her car.

Eliza parked and peered over at her.

"Hey!" Her mom said, shutting the trunk of her car and giving her a hug. "I didn't know you were coming home this weekend!"

"Yeah." She let out a breath. "I have some news."

"Something exciting?"

Eliza pulled back. "Exciting for the guys who just bought our couch, yes."

Her smile fell. "Oh no, what happened? Is Cora okay?"

"She's fine. Except for the past six months she's been taking our rent money and going shopping. We got evicted."

She gasped. "That's awful!"

"I know."

Why couldn't she ever make her mom proud? Why couldn't she bring good news, or something fun? Why did she endlessly spin her tires, only sinking lower and lower?

"I'm sorry I'm such a failure," Eliza added with a sigh.

"You are *not* a failure!" Her mom said firmly, putting an arm around her. "What about tea? Do you want some tea? Let's go inside."

They walked into the house and Eliza took a seat on one of the kitchen stools. "I'll need to stay with you for a bit, if that's okay."

"That's more than okay. I'm thrilled! Really, honey. It's not all that tragic. I'm a good roommate."

The best Eliza could do was grunt. She disagreed – it *was* that tragic – but she didn't want to induce a full-blown pep talk from her mom.

"There is one little thing. I have news, too."

Eliza clapped a hand to her mouth. "I almost forgot! The promotion!"

Her mom set a water kettle to boil. "No, not that. I've decided to make a change. I'm going to live with Granny for a few weeks. Maybe a few months. I don't know."

"On the island?" Eliza's mouth dropped open. "I'm so jealous!"

"Come with me!" Mom said with a laugh. "Granny needs help with the tea shop, and honestly, with everything else, too. I'm sure she'd love to have you stay with her, and we could use a lot of help on the tea shop's website."

"No. I can't." Eliza was going to give a reason, but she couldn't come up with one.

What did she have to lose? She'd already lost her apartment. She needed time away from her best friend, and her job was the least important thing in her life.

"Actually..." Eliza tilted her head. "I could."

Her mom clapped her hands together. "Really? We'll have so much fun!"

Something wasn't adding up. She eyed her mom warily. "What made you decide to do this?"

"A lot of things." She set two mugs on the kitchen counter. "I'll tell you when you're older."

"*Mom.* That doesn't work on me anymore. I'm not a kid."

"Yeah, but you're still *my* kid." She smiled. "It's just – Granny needs some help. She told me she was thinking of moving to a nursing home."

"*What!* But Granny's so wild! I never thought she'd leave the island. Maybe to like, live on a cruise ship again. Or to run a safari."

Her mom laughed. "I know. She's slowed down in the past few years, though. We're all getting older."

Eliza looked down at her hands. How could twenty-four feel so old? "I know."

"I was thinking of renting the house out while we're away. What do you think?"

Eliza made a face. "With people touching our stuff? Sleeping in our beds? I don't know. It's kind of gross."

Her mom was quiet for a moment. "Yeah. That's a good point. We can figure it out later."

She poured the boiling water into mugs and slid one over to Eliza, along with a box of tea bags.

She picked a bag of Lady Grey and dipped it into the water. "When are you going up?"

"I just came home to do a few things and pack, so soon! I need to tell your sisters. Hopefully they won't mind."

Her sisters had lives that were going places. Why would they mind?

The mug warmed her hands, and the gentle tones of bergamot drifted to her nose.

"I think it'll be fine." She took a sip of tea. "My car is already packed with all my stuff. Maybe I'll just go up now."

"Give Granny a call. She'll be ecstatic."

Eliza couldn't help but smile. There were *two* people happy about her leaving her apartment. Not bad, in the grand scheme of things.

She looked up. "I will."

For the first time in months, she felt excited. An adventure on San Juan Island? Why hadn't she thought of that before?

Thirteen

After one call to Patty, Eliza was on her way, grinning ear to ear. Sheila stood outside in her slippers to wave as she backed out of the driveway.

She couldn't believe how quickly Eliza's mood had transformed. Sheila hadn't seen her so happy in, well, years.

It wasn't fair. Sheila used to think the hardest part of raising kids was when they were little. She was wrong. When they were small, she could solve their problems and ease their pains. When they got older, all she could do was watch, listen, and worry.

Eliza hadn't had an easy road. She struggled after the divorce, and though she'd deny it, her damaged relationship with her dad played a big part in her decision to drop out of school.

Sheila couldn't think about it without getting upset. Brian had decided the girls didn't need him as much as he needed to run off and find himself. It made her want to call and yell at him again.

When Cora had suggested moving in with Eliza, it was a blessing at first. Cora had known Eliza from childhood; she knew her moods and her tendency to overthink and spiral.

She'd drag her out of bed to go dancing or decorate her room with Christmas lights when she was feeling down.

Recently, though, things had taken a turn. As generous as Cora was, she was wildly irresponsible. Her spending was out of control, and poor Eliza couldn't tell her no, even when Cora was stealing the rent to fund her lifestyle.

It's hard to abandon the ones we love, even when they're hurting us. Maybe especially so. Sheila knew that as well as anyone, so she didn't blame Eliza, but she thought it would be good for them to have a break.

Even better, they'd all get to live together at the cottage. Sheila couldn't wait to join them.

There was just one thing she had to do first.

It wasn't anything responsible; nothing she should be doing, like figuring out if she could rent the house or looking for a job.

Nothing to do with the adult responsibilities she was ignoring and everything to do with a promise she'd made as a nine-year-old girl.

Sheila walked inside and locked the door behind her. She needed to make sure she was alone. She'd buried this part of her so deep that she'd never even told Brian about it.

She got to the kitchen, stopped at the counter, and laughed out loud. If Brian knew about this, he'd think *she* was having a midlife crisis.

But maybe it was her turn! Maybe letting this secret haunt her forever wasn't an option. When she'd found out Lottie was alive, it felt like something had physically hit her in the chest. She started dreaming of her, hearing the cries in her sleep.

Then when she heard about Tokitae, it was more than a punch. She was the whale from the news clipping, the last believed living captive resident orca.

Her death had been a tragedy, and to Sheila it was even more. It was a sign. Sheila *had* to do something. She couldn't let Lottie suffer the same fate, dying alone in a tank miles and miles from home, impossibly far from her family.

After being assigned to work on the Marine Magic Funland account, Sheila had dug deep and quickly discovered no one knew the truth about Lottie.

They knew her name, but they thought she'd been caught in international waters. No one knew she was one of the endangered southern resident whales. No one knew her family was still alive out there, waiting for her.

Sheila learned everything she could about the business – how it was suffering and wouldn't survive three more years with their current revenue and expenses, how they'd brought in two new partners to little relief, how Lottie's tank was leaking, how the roller coasters needed substantial service, and how they were down to one security guard for overnights.

Oh yes, she'd learned *a lot* in her time there, like the guard going on vacation that weekend. He'd loudly complained that the security cameras didn't work, that no one appreciated him, and they'd better hope nothing happened while he was gone.

Sheila walked out to her car, got the pink box, and carried it inside the house. After locking the door, she opened it and stared at the contents, all just as she'd left them.

She'd never committed a burglary before. She'd never even stolen candy from the store as a kid. This wasn't going to be easy.

Sheila was a humble woman. She knew she couldn't steal a whale, but she had to find a way to help. She was the only person left who could prove who Lottie really was – prove to everyone that this orca belonged back in the ocean with her family.

Her plan was too mad to speak aloud to another human being, but Sheila wasn't going to let that stop her. She looked at the contents of the box one more time before snapping it shut.

It was now or never.

.   .   .

She waited until dark, then drove to a shopping mall half a mile from Marine Magic Funland. She parked her car in the far end of the lot, then took the bakery box out of her trunk and disappeared into the woods.

There was no trail, but she was prepared, using the compass app on her phone. If it weren't such an absurd situation, she might've felt kind of cool.

It took ten minutes of carefully creeping through the forest to reach the back of the whale stadium. Under the cover of the trees, Sheila set the bakery box down and took out her supplies, pulling on the ski mask, the gloves, and looping the rope and rappelling gear over her shoulder.

She knew from the security guard that there was a chainlink fence in the back that was ten feet high, and in his eyes, far too easy to climb.

A few lights were still on at the stadium, and she could see clearly. Sheila crept along until she reached the fence. All she had to do was throw the rope over and –

Hang on. She stood from her crouched position, squinting. Were her eyes fooling her? Or was the gate standing ajar?

She moved closer, listening for the sound of voices or footsteps. After a full minute, she hadn't heard anything, and she dropped the rope and rappelling gear onto the ground. With the sound of her thundering heart in her ears, she quietly slipped through the open gate.

She didn't make a sound, and no alarms rang out.

She kept walking, reaching the back of the tank beneath ground level. There was a large viewing window where she could see inside. Lottie had already taken notice of her. She swam over to the window and paused, hanging in the water as Sheila stood in front of the glowing blue window, her mouth hanging open.

"Hey girl," she whispered, putting her gloved hand up to the window.

Lottie stared back at her with the eye Sheila remembered so well – even then, she seemed old and wise. They watched one another for what felt like an eternity.

Then, without warning, Lottie swam off.

"Wait!" Sheila yelled, then sucked in a sharp breath, chastising herself.

She still needed to be quiet. There could be someone here.

She stood and listened. The only sound she heard was Lottie taking a breath at the surface of the water.

Sheila crept around the tank, walking past the trainer area, past the rows of plastic buckets, and jumped over a small barrier to get to the side of the tank with audience seating.

Here there was tall plexiglass siding, and Lottie returned, gliding by the glass once, then spinning around with stunning grace to return.

Sheila laughed. "Do you remember me?"

It occurred to her how ridiculous that question was, not only because she was talking to a whale, but because she was wearing a ski mask. She looked over her shoulder, then, convinced she was alone, carefully pulled the mask up to the top of her head. "I'm bigger now, but it's still me."

Lottie came closer. *She* was so much bigger, the length of a two-story house. The size her mother had been.

Sheila walked along the side of the tank and Lottie followed. She hopped a barrier and easily got into the trainer area, standing at the water's edge.

Lottie came to the surface, her black skin shining in the moonlight. She was close enough for Sheila to reach out a hand and touch her...

Not that she dared. "I'm going to play something for you, and I want you to listen."

Lottie stayed, patiently waiting with her head out of the water.

Good. She understood.

Sheila pulled up the file on her phone, the one she'd gotten after emailing an orca researcher. It was a recording of orca calls from the three southern resident pods.

Sheila had never known how complicated orcas were. Each of the three pods had a distinct dialect, and the researcher said she could differentiate them based on recordings alone.

"And the orcas know who they're talking to, too?"

The woman had written back with an enthusiastic, "Of course! They recognize one another just as easily as you and I would!"

Sheila hit play, the sound from her phone filling the empty stadium. Lottie turned onto her side and gently lifted her flipper out of the water, holding it as though she was reaching out.

Sheila played three one-minute clips. Lottie had no reaction to the first two, but with the third, she immediately started whistling and clicking.

"Did you understand that? Did you know what they were saying?"

Lottie fell silent, but Sheila could hardly contain her excitement. The last recording was from the L-pod group of whales. Was it possible this was her family? Would it be enough to prove that she was actually a southern resident whale? Would it be enough to convince the failing business to let her go?

"Hang on a second. I need to record you." Sheila fumbled with her phone. Her hands were cold from nerves, but she managed to hit record.

For thirty seconds, Lottie didn't make a peep, but just as Sheila started to wonder if she was making it all up in her head, Lottie started calling out again.

This went on for a full minute, ending with an enthusiastic call and Lottie launching herself halfway out of the water.

The sudden motion startled Sheila, and she jumped, dropping her phone into the water with a *plop*.

Her stomach sank. "No, no, no, no," she whispered, rushing down the stairs and kneeling near the window, watching as her phone elegantly swooped and sank to the bottom of the tank.

Lottie fell silent, bobbing beneath the surface and watching Sheila through the glass.

After a moment, she dipped low, swimming to the bottom of the tank and delicately grabbing the phone.

Sheila watched, her mouth hanging open, as Lottie swam back to the surface at the trainer's stage.

She seemed to be waiting for her.

Did she dare get *that* close? What was the chance Lottie would pull her in? Surely she didn't appreciate a stranger waking her up and tramping around her tank in the middle of the night...

At the same time, Sheila needed that phone. She needed the recording, and she couldn't leave behind any evidence that she'd been here.

She went back up the stairs and carefully walked onto the stage. It sloped into the pool, with water gently washing up.

Lottie was still waiting, her mouth open, the phone balanced on the edge of her teeth. Sheila took a breath to steady herself. She squatted, then slowly leaned forward and took the phone from Lottie's mouth.

As soon as she was clear, she jumped back, the blood rushing back to her limbs.

"Thank you," she said.

Lottie popped up from the water, clicking and squeaking, and Sheila smiled.

She knew she should be more afraid, but the longer she looked at Lottie, the more at ease she felt.

Sheila dropped to her knees, her black jeans absorbing the cold water. "Let's see if my phone still works. Do you want to hear it again?"

Lottie turned on her side, looking at her, and Sheila laughed. "Okay, let me try."

Amazingly, after wiping it off on her sleeve, her phone started as if nothing had happened. She played the clip of L-pod again, and Lottie floated only a few inches away, listening.

A booming voice broke Sheila from her awe. "Hey! Get out of there!"

She shoved the phone in her pocket and stood, turning to run and falling instantly, like a character in a children's cartoon. She hit the concrete hard with her hip, water soaking into her clothes, but she stood again, stumbling, running back to the gate.

She could hear the man yelling, but it didn't sound like the guard she knew. She wasn't about to look back and see; she could hear his footsteps gaining on her.

Sheila burst through the fence gate and disappeared into the darkness of the forest, running as fast as her feet would take her.

Fourteen

Patty couldn't believe her good luck. What had seemed like the end – her little spotted cottage garnering the wrong kind of attention – was only the beginning! First, Sheila announced she was moving in with her, and now Eliza had shown up, looking for a place to stay, too!

To top it all off, the devilishly handsome Russell Westwood showed up at her door that Sunday with a pair of gardening gloves and a wagon filled with little lavender plants.

"You asked for it," he said when she opened the door. "Here I am. Ready to work."

"I was only joking!" Patty said, both hands on her face in surprise. "Please, come in. I'll make you something."

He shook his head. "Sorry, Miss Dennet. You said you wanted me to pull weeds, and that's what I'm here for."

Patty stuck her head out the door, peering around the corner. "Should I expect a camera crew to show up? 'Famous actor helps little old lady who can't maintain her home'?"

"Not unless you're the one who called them," he said with a laugh.

Eliza came flying down the stairs. "Who are you talking to, Granny?"

"Russell Westwood."

"Ha ha, very funny. I wanted to –" She stopped when she reached the doorway, her mouth hanging open. "You're Russell Westwood."

"I am. And you are...Sheila's daughter?"

"You know my mom?"

"Not well, no. We just met, but I can see the resemblance."

"This is my granddaughter, Eliza. She's coming to stay with me, too. You've just gained *two* new neighbors. You'd think they might be moving here for you, but they're moving here for me!" Patty cackled, unable to contain her joy. "Maybe you should call that TV crew after all. I'm very popular!"

Russell smiled. "I didn't mean to interrupt your family time. I'm here to work. Is there anywhere in particular you'd like me to start?"

She put her hands on her hips. "I can't let you do this."

"I'll go where I see fit, then." He smiled and nodded a goodbye before walking off.

"Honestly," she muttered, closing the front door. "If I'd known he was going to come over, I could've put together a garden picnic or something."

"Granny," Eliza said slowly, "Why didn't you tell me *Russell Westwood* was your neighbor?"

"There's been so much excitement, I forgot! I thought your mom would tell you."

That wasn't a good sign. Maybe Sheila wasn't as charmed with him as she hoped she would be...

Or maybe it was just Sheila being Sheila. Playing hard to get – no, hard to crack.

What would it take for her to entertain the idea of love again?

Patty thought she would never love again after her first husband died. She raised the boys on her own, and when they grew up, she quite happily filled her life with friends and hobbies and travel.

Then she'd met Ray. She was sure it wasn't possible for her to have *two* great loves in her life, but there he was, even more wonderful than he even seemed.

When he passed away, she knew she'd been lucky. There was no need to get greedy. Besides, she was too heartbroken to even entertain the idea of romance. And too old! What was she going to do, join a dating website for seniors?

It was too absurd. She was happy to have her cottage and her family.

But then Reggie walked into her life. They'd found such a quiet happiness she didn't know was possible. It made her believe that anyone, absolutely *anyone*, could find love. It only made her more determined to find someone for Sheila.

"Mom definitely did not mention the famous actor living next door!" Eliza said. "I can't believe this! What else haven't you told me? Is Oprah coming over for brunch?"

"Wouldn't that be fun?" Patty stopped. "There's an idea. Brunch! Your mom should be here soon." Her mind started turning. She had everything she needed for a nice meal, though a picnic might be iffy with the rain forecast.

Eliza peered out the window. "He's just...pulling weeds out there. Russell Westwood is pulling weeds in your garden."

"Why don't you go get my gardening gloves and keep him company?" Patty suggested, pushing her down the hall.

"Keep Russell Westwood company? There's no way! I went into shock the second I saw him. It's embarrassing."

"You're not a big talker anyway," Patty said, waving a hand. "Take my hat, too. It looks like rain."

"Granny. I'm not doing this."

"What else were you going to do today? Hm?"

"You know, I was thinking of..." Her voice trailed off, and she peered through the window again. "What's he like?"

"He's very nice," she said simply. "I think he's lonely."

Eliza kept staring through the window, her eyes wide.

"You can't just watch him like an animal at the zoo!" Patty said. She found her gardening gloves and shoved them into Eliza's hands. "Don't be afraid of him. It's not like he's Idris Elba. It's just Russell."

"Just Russell!" Eliza said with a laugh. "Right. You're on a first-name basis with him."

"You will be too if you'll *just go outside.*" Patty gave another helpful push toward the door. "This is your life. Go and live it!"

Eliza groaned, but then miraculously said, "Fine. But only because it needs to be done."

"There's a shovel in the shed. Watch out for spider webs!" Patty called out before rushing back to the kitchen to get started on her newly hatched plan for brunch.

In under an hour, she had pulled it together. The timing was perfect, and Sheila arrived just as she set the water for tea.

"Perfect timing!" she yelled from the open kitchen window. "Everyone, come inside and wash up. It looks like the rain is holding off, so we can eat on the back patio."

She was quite pleased with what she'd thrown together. It was simple, but pretty all laid out: a smashed potato frittata, deviled eggs, smoked salmon on toast, and sausage stuffed honey buns she'd made for Reggie two weeks ago and frozen the leftovers.

When she returned to the table with a teapot, she was happy to see Eliza's stage fright had melted. She and Russell were laughing together.

"What's so funny?" Patty asked.

"Just Russell making fun of me for talking to worms."

"Not making fun," he said, his face solemn. "Trying to learn the lingo. *Hang tight, little dude, you'll be in good dirt again soon.*'"

They broke into laughter as Sheila walked onto the back porch.

She looked a bit worse for the wear, with bags under her eyes and her hair in a rough ponytail.

"Is everything okay?" Patty asked in a low voice.

She nodded. "I'll tell you later."

Everyone enjoyed the brunch, and Russell didn't miss a beat in reminding Sheila what she'd promised him. "I was hoping that maybe sometime this or next week we can meet up to talk about my finances?"

She flashed a smile. "Of course. I'd be happy to."

His phone rang and he frowned. "Speaking of, that's my business partner. This was great. Thank you for the impromptu brunch. Will you ladies excuse me?"

Patty beamed up at him. "Of course. Thank you again for coming."

He smiled, then answered the call as he walked off, crossing the invisible boundary between their properties.

Sheila let out a groan. "I thought he'd never leave."

"Sheila!" Patty threw her napkin down. "Russell is a nice man! You can't hold it against him that he's rich and –"

Sheila cut her off. "I need to talk to you. Both of you."

My goodness, she was serious. "What's the matter?"

"I've done something reckless."

Eliza smiled. "Yeah sure, Mom. Like that one time you said you were going to live on the wild side and you declined the rental car insurance?"

A faint smile crossed Sheila's face. "No. Not like that."

"Did you go and yell at another neighbor?" Patty asked, then laughed at her own joke.

"No." Sheila let out a sigh and dropped her voice. "I think I might be getting arrested soon."

Fifteen

H e hated to leave the table just then, but his business partner had called three times. Something was up. Russell waited to answer until he was out of earshot.

"Harry, what's going on?"

Maybe if it was a quick conversation, he could go back to Patty's. Maybe he could get Sheila to speak to him, or just *look* at him. He'd take her yelling at him. Anything, really, to be the focus of her mesmerizing intensity again.

It made him feel...well, *something*. He wasn't quite sure what it was, but after hiding for the past few years, it was something he couldn't stop thinking about.

"We've had a bit of excitement at Funland," Harry said. "Nothing to worry you, and nothing that will cost you money."

Russell laughed. That was good because he didn't plan on spending any more money on the park. Buying partial ownership had been Holly's idea. She'd shot a movie there, a thriller called *Race on a Roller Coaster Heart*, and after the movie was successful, she felt sentimental about the park. The owner offered to let her become a part owner, and she had taken the deal.

During the divorce, he couldn't understand why she gave it to him as an asset. Now, after dealing with all the unexpected bills and years of deferred maintenance, he understood it hadn't been a gift.

"Someone broke into the whale stadium last night," Harry said, quickly adding, "Nothing was taken, and nothing was broken. Lottie's okay, too."

"Ah, man," Russell covered his eyes with his hand. "That's a huge liability, Harry. We can't have people getting into the park at night and getting themselves hurt."

"I know, and it's being taken care of."

"What were they doing? Did they catch him?"

"Not yet, and who knows? We have camera footage, but we can't make out the person's face. We've got a team working on it. They're going to beef up our security and track this person down."

"All right. Well, keep me updated, I guess."

They ended the call and Russell took a seat on one of his patio chairs. He felt bad, but what was he supposed to do? He had no control over how the park ran.

In truth, he'd wanted to sell off his ownership, but he couldn't find anyone to buy it.

It was something he could talk to Sheila about: how to unload this asset. It could be part of a bigger conversation about how to put his financial life back together.

Perhaps he'd been too passive in the divorce. He didn't really fight with Holly for anything. He should've, at the very least, made her keep this park. But he hadn't.

She'd always handled all the money, told him what they could and couldn't afford. Since Holly had left, he'd made some big purchases – a home outside of Yellowstone. A new truck. An investment into a documentary. Repairs at the park. He was, truthfully, afraid to look at his expenses. Afraid to see what sort of financial trajectory he was on. It didn't feel like it was going well, and if he faced it, he might have to do another movie. That was impossible.

Sheila could look out for him. She could give him the bad news, tell him what he had to sell off. Whatever she told him, he would do. He trusted her not to sugarcoat or lie or to try to get anything from him.

The thought startled him and he turned away from the vast ocean view.

It had been years since he felt like he could trust someone. It was a good sign. She could be his financial advisor. It was another perk of moving here – meeting non-Hollywood types.

Yeah, that was all. He got up and went back home.

Sixteen

Patty and Eliza were staring at her. There was no going back now. Sheila had to tell them what she'd done...and what she'd not done.

It was important for Eliza to understand her mom was human. Eliza suffered from the curse of youth, thinking she was the only flawed one, the only broken one. Calling herself a failure – which was simply not the case!

Sheila made mistakes too, as she'd proven in this month of madness.

She looked around. The coast was clear, with no one but the seabirds to overhear her story. She took a deep breath and started from the beginning: her mother leaving, her dad capturing Lottie and selling her off.

She went on, telling them how, on her birthday this year, she'd heard about Tokitae's death, how the guilt kept her up at night and drove her to madness. About the burglary box, how she'd gotten herself fired from her job and, finally, how nearly got caught committing a break-in.

When she was done, she sat back and waited to be scolded.

"Mom, that is *so* cool!" Eliza said. "I can't believe you did that!"

"I can't believe you kept it to yourself for so long," Patty said. "Normally you can't keep a secret to save your life."

Sheila crossed her arms. "Oh, I'm sorry I'm not more like the woman who never told us how much she was struggling until she almost had to move out."

Patty waved a hand. "That was nothing. Just typical life stuff. Now *this!*" She tapped a finger on the table. "*This* is something. It's a story. You should tell Russell. Have him turn it into a movie."

"No one is telling Russell!" Sheila said, cutting her off. "Don't tell *anyone* about this. I mean it." She turned to Eliza. "I'm going to tell your sisters, of course. I just have to find the right time."

Patty started gathering plates, but when Sheila stood to help, she slapped her hand away. "Please let me take care of my own home."

Sheila ignored her and started stacking cups. "Let me help while I can. Before I go to prison."

"Oh hush!" Patty laughed, balancing a serving plate on the top of the stack. "It's not even serious. You didn't steal anything! What's that, a charge for trespassing? That's nothing."

"Nothing?" Sheila dropped her voice to a whisper. "I had a *burglary box* in my car. I presented it to my boss! Everyone saw it!"

A laugh burst from Eliza. "*Please* let me tell Mackenzie. She'll die laughing."

Sheila shot her an exasperated look. "No, don't do that. I'm just saying, Patty. It certainly feels like something."

A grin spread across Patty's face. "Yes. It feels like the Sheila I've missed is finally back."

She grabbed the teapot with her free hand and sauntered back to the cottage.

Sheila followed, her arms full. As much as she wanted to resent Patty's teasing, she couldn't help but smile a little.

Yes, running through the woods had been terrifying, and her hip really hurt, and what she'd done was terribly irresponsible, but at the same time, she hadn't felt so alive in years.

She dropped the dishes off in the kitchen and returned to the table. Eliza was busy wiping up crumbs.

"Can you believe I just pulled weeds with Russell Westwood?" she said, straightening and shaking her head. "I mean, I know you're busy with your exciting life of crime, but isn't that insane?"

"It is," Sheila admitted. She'd hardly had time to reflect on it or feel self-conscious about being around him.

"Do you remember when we went to see him in *Hearts under the Rhododendron*? I was in love with him for like three years."

Sheila laughed. "I hope you told him about that."

"No." She rolled her eyes. "I'm way over that. He's too old. He's your age!" She froze and made a face. "No offense."

"None taken." Russell didn't look old to Sheila. He looked picture-perfect, like he'd been cut out of a magazine, with his piercing blue eyes and chiseled features.

If he wasn't old, then maybe that meant she wasn't old either?

"Do you know who Granny's celebrity crush is?" Sheila asked.

Before Eliza could answer, Patty emerged from the cottage with a dish rag on her shoulder. "What's the matter with you two? I said leave it!"

Sheila felt like she'd recovered from purging her secrets and decided to have a little fun with Patty's. "Have you told Eliza about the new man in your life?"

A scowl settled onto her face. "What? What man? There's no man. There are no men in my life."

Eliza raised her eyebrows. "You mean Idris Elba?"

Patty's mouth popped open, and Sheila and Eliza burst into hysterics.

Patty let out a tut as she wiped down the table. "You two," she muttered, hiding a smile.

Eliza smiled and turned back to tidying up.

It lifted Sheila's soul to hear Eliza laugh. She'd grown so serious in the last few years, so hard to reach. Sheila knew she was unhappy. She could feel it in her long silences, see it in her sullen eyes.

Sheila would do anything to make her daughter happy, but there was not much she could do. Now that she had come to the cottage, something already felt different. This was the right place for all of them. There was something healing about it. She had a real chance to help Patty, and Eliza, and even Lottie.

Maybe, if she was lucky, she could help herself a little, too.

. . .

They spent the rest of the evening trying to convince Patty to let them inside the tea shop. She didn't break down until just before her eight o'clock bedtime.

"All right, all right. Tomorrow morning, I'll let you both in to see it. But no teasing about what a disaster it is. I'm serious. I can't bear it."

Sheila and Eliza promised not to tease, and the next morning, after Patty served a very full breakfast, she slowly walked them over to the tea shop.

"It would break Ray's heart to see it shuttered like this," she said. "It got to the point where I thought if I didn't go inside, I could convince myself it was just closed for a long weekend."

"Hm," Eliza said. "Denial. I use that all the time. I didn't know it was a family trait."

"I'm sure it's not that bad," Sheila said, but she prepared herself for the worst.

The outside of the building didn't look too rough – not as rundown as the cottage. It was a more recently touched structure, updated by Ray himself to fulfill Patty's lifelong dream of running a tea shop.

Growing up, Patty's military father had been stationed all over the world – South Korea, Japan, London, and even Poland for a brief spat. Young Patty had thrived on going from place to place, and her hippy soul soared, fascinated by the people she met and the places she saw. She was especially interested in how tea mattered in each culture and dreamed of running a shop of her own one day.

When she and Ray had moved to the island, he'd vowed to build her the tea shop of her dreams. It was a humble building – one level with an entryway, a small kitchen, and three tea rooms.

The first room was London-themed, another was Japanese style, and the last tearoom was designed for children.

That had always been Sheila's favorite. There were cartoon characters painted on the walls, scenes around campfires, and whimsical moons and stars. Patty had made a special menu with hot chocolate, cookies, and miniature s'mores cooked over little candles.

When they had first opened, it was magical, and their offerings had been quite popular. People had raved about enjoying tea on the patio with a gorgeous view of the water.

Sheila knew that for Patty to abandon this dream, it had to have been quite bad. She braced herself as they reached the front door. Patty's hand shook as she unlocked it.

"I can't go in," she said, shoving the keys in her coat pocket. "You go. I'll be at the cottage. I'm making the Jennifer Aniston salad I emailed you about. Did you see it? The recipe? They said she ate it all the time when she was shooting *Friends.*"

Sheila shook her head. "I don't think so, but I'm sure it's lovely."

"Fresh mint and parsley, that's the key," Patty called out as she walked away. "I've got good lemons for it, too."

They watched her make her way back to the cottage. Eliza turned to Sheila. "Poor Granny."

She sighed. "I know. Let's take a look."

She pushed the door open and they walked inside. There was dust and spiderwebs, which she had expected, but otherwise, it looked tidy. Sunlight streamed through the windows onto an apron hanging behind the cash register, as though waiting to be put into service at any moment.

Sheila walked back toward the kitchen and pushed the swinging door. The sink was clean, a dry rag hanging on the edge. All the teacups and teapots were in their places.

She turned and went into the kids' tearoom. There was thick dust on every surface, but the paintings were as cute as ever, and the view from the windows was stunning.

They could see the patio now, and Sheila peered through the window, taking note of everything. Weeds had covered most of the stone, and the tables and chairs were rusty, but with the ocean sparkling behind it, the scene was still magnificent.

"It honestly isn't that bad," Eliza said, walking in behind her. "It's kind of creepy, being empty like this, but I think if we got some new light bulbs, cleaned up, and repainted, it'd be perfect."

Sheila ran a hand on the booth seat. They'd visited the tea shop with the girls so many times. Eliza had been a teenager then, but she had still relished toasting marshmallows for her little sisters.

"Granny said there's something wrong with the insurance. I'll sort that out, and maybe we can be back up and running in a few weeks," Sheila said.

"I found the tea list!" Eliza said, holding up a thick black binder. Each page was laminated and had a description of the tea, where it came from, how it paired best. "I can redo these and get them on the website."

"There's no website," Sheila said with a smile. "Remember?"

Eliza cracked a smile. "Oh. I'll make one, then. We can host events! Like movie nights on the patio. We can get one of those big outdoor screens. And music nights! Open mics. You could play something."

She let out a laugh. "I don't think that's a good idea."

"Why not? Dad's not here anymore. He can't get mad at you for it."

Sheila's gaze halted and she turned to her daughter. "That's – that's not it."

"Yes it is. Dad always got mad about your music."

"No, honey, it wasn't –"

"I'm not blind, Mom. And I'm not a little kid anymore."

She smiled at her. "Believe me, I know."

"Dad was always weird about your music. I think he was jealous."

It was unbelievable the things kids picked up. Brian wasn't jealous – well, maybe he had been, at some level. Threatened, in a way. Any success Sheila had with her music was a threat to the balance of their lives, the balance where Sheila's career took a backseat to his, where her best moments were their biggest fights.

A man's voice called out. "Hello?"

She shot Eliza an alarmed look, but Eliza was smiling.

"Come on in!" her daughter yelled, then dropped her voice. "It's Russell! I invited him."

"You *invited* him?" Sheila whispered back.

Eliza shrugged. "What? He's helpful, and I thought you might need a friend."

"I don't need friends."

"Come on, Mom," Eliza whispered, "how often do you get to hang out with a movie star?"

"Hey there!" Russell said, stepping into the doorway. "I hope I'm not interrupting anything."

Before Sheila could react, Eliza spoke up. "Not at all! We were just figuring out what we needed to do to get this place back up and running."

"It's really nice in here," he said, looking around. "Do you need help? I'm pretty handy, and I can fill any of my knowledge gaps with instructional YouTube videos."

"No, that's all right," Sheila said quickly.

"That would be amazing, actually," Eliza contradicted. "Do you have a ladder? I think we need to repaint most of these walls, and the trim, and the ceilings. I want to get all the light bulbs replaced too, because the yellow lighting isn't really working for me."

Sheila turned to her with wide eyes. "When did you decide we were going to do all of that?"

She shrugged. "While I was walking around."

"I'm happy to help," Russell said.

Eliza beamed at Sheila expectantly, but all she could manage was a grunt.

"Thank you for that," Eliza said. "If you'll excuse me, I'm going to take a look at the teacups."

Eliza disappeared, and Sheila was left staring at Russell. The weight of his celebrity really hit her now.

He was at ease, though, looking around and surveying the room. "My kids would've loved this when they were little."

Sheila cleared her throat. "Yeah, it was always a hit with my girls."

He turned to face her. "I hope I'm not making myself too much of a nuisance."

"Of course not," Sheila heard herself say.

"It's been slow going, making friends on the island. Actually," he rubbed the back of his neck with his hand, "ever since the divorce, really. Life hasn't really been the same."

She knew he was divorced, but she'd resisted looking up any details. It was easier to imagine other people's divorces as they were described in polite company. "Things didn't work out," or "We wanted different things." She didn't want to imagine the open wounds beneath those statements.

"Divorce does that to a person," she said.

"Yeah." He laughed. "For so long, I wanted to be alone. That's where the wolves came in."

Sheila let out a little laugh. "Right. The wolves. How could I forget about the wolves?"

He shook his head. "I don't know. I never forget about them. I'm kind of insulted you have already."

"Wolf 12 is my guy," Sheila said.

Russell stared at her, his mouth in a flat line. "I thought you loved Wolf 8."

"Oh, right." A laugh burst out of her. "Wolf 8, my hero."

"Is this a joke to you?" he asked, crossing his arms. "I bet you can't even tell Wolf 8 and Wolf 21 apart."

"I bet *you* can't tell them apart," Sheila said lamely, her laughter building even more.

"I have more pictures of Wolf 21 on my wall than I do my own children," he said firmly. "How *dare* you."

Now she was doubled over. She didn't know why – maybe because he was a world-famous actor – but his delivery was hilarious.

When she finally ran out of steam, she put up a hand. "Okay, I'm sorry. You win. I don't know about wolves. You caught me."

"It's okay." He let out a heavy sigh. "I'll be able to tell you all about them when we're repainting the walls. I have a ladder, you know."

"You really don't have to help. Don't listen to Eliza. She can get so bossy, but –"

"No. Please." He smiled that dazzling movie-star smile. "It's not even for Patty. It's for you."

Her heart leapt and her breath ran out. She managed to quickly recover. "For me?"

"Yes. Your wolf knowledge is abysmal. If you're going to pull off that howling-at-the-moon wardrobe, you need some help."

Ah, of course. She smiled. "I'll make sure to wear that shirt on our first day working."

His expression brightened. "Can't wait."

Seventeen

R emodeling a tea shop hadn't been on his bingo card for the year, but Russell couldn't be happier. It gave him something to do, and he felt like he was becoming part of the community, particularly with Patty shouting at them through the windows and preparing daily lunches.

Both he and Sheila worked under Eliza's guidance. She was a serious young woman, which he appreciated, and it only made it more fun to break through her focus and get her to laugh.

"This isn't a comedy!" she barked at him.

"What is it, then? I need more direction," he said.

"It's a coming-of-age story."

Sheila made a face. "For whom?"

"The tea shop, of course," Eliza said before flitting away and leaving them to their painting.

He stole a glance at Sheila, but her eyes were fixed on her paintbrush, delicately outlining white trim. They'd spent a week and a half doing a deep clean and repainting the walls and ceilings, and now all that was left were the details.

He turned back to his work, painting the edges of the ceiling as "Harness Your Hopes" played in the background.

Sheila crafted their daily playlists, and he had no complaints. For the last two days it had been '90's indie rock, with Heatmiser, The Breeders, and the Pixies on heavy rotation.

Until this point, Sheila had spent much of their time together skillfully steering the conversation away from herself. She had zeroed in on his weak spot – wolves – and asked question after question.

Today, however, he was determined to talk about something else. "Did Patty make you watch *Grey's Anatomy* last night?"

"Of course," Sheila said with a smile. "But I was thinking about Wolf 21."

Russell looked over at her. "No, you weren't."

"I was. Why would he join a rival pack where the alpha female was so vicious?"

Just when he thought she had to be humoring him, she had to go and make a thoughtful comment about Wolf 21.

"Wolves are individuals, just like me or you. They have their own personalities and histories." It was too late now; he couldn't stop. He set his paintbrush down. "They make choices about how to live their lives."

"Right," she said. "I was reading about Wolf 8 last night during the show – much to Patty's annoyance."

He laughed. "I can imagine."

She smiled, her eyes still focused on the trim. "He was the runt, right? They thought he was going to starve to death or be run off by his brothers."

"Yeah, but there was more to him than his size. He stood up to a full-grown bear and scared it off. He found a starving mother with eight pups and saved them, raising the pups as his own."

"One of them was Wolf 21. His step-wolf."

Russell laughed. She was at least a little interested. "Yes, and Wolf 21 learned everything from Wolf 8. He learned his compassion. He grew to be huge and strong, but even when 21 pinned a rival wolf and they were completely defeated, he never killed them."

"He raised another wolf's pups too, didn't he?"

"He did. He was an extraordinary wolf."

Russell cleared his throat. If she got him going again, he'd spend the whole day talking about the Yellowstone wolves.

He wasn't here to talk about wolves, though. There was no such thing as a lone wolf, and he couldn't be one either.

Russell did the only thing he could think of: he asked her a boring question that people had probably asked her a million times.

"Anyway. What made you want to get into accounting?"

Sheila shrugged. "I'm just a boring person."

"I don't believe that."

She set her paintbrush down. "What made you get into acting? Did you look in the mirror one day and decide you were just really, really good-looking and everyone needed to see?"

He laughed. She was not going to make it easy to get to know her. "Yes, that's what exactly happened."

"Knew it," Sheila said with a smirk.

Russell cleared his throat. "It was actually because of a girl. I was trying to impress her. She was a drama major. I auditioned for *Hamlet* and got a part."

"Ah, and *then* you looked in the mirror?"

Relentless teasing. His favorite kind of teasing. "Not exactly. A talent scout spotted me. He was visiting Minnesota for Christmas and convinced me to move to LA."

She paused what she was doing to look at him. "Wait, you were discovered? That sounds made up."

"I know." He laughed. "But it's true. I took a bunch of acting classes and I loved it. I loved conveying a story, you know?"

She bit her lip and looked down. "Hm. Even though I've never acted, I think I know what you mean."

"That was when I moved in with Hank. Er, Henry Rattler."

She put a hand over her mouth. "Wait, that's right! You've been in a bunch of his movies."

Russell studied her for a moment. Sometimes people pretended not to know about his past, as if it weren't available with a quick internet search.

But Sheila's surprise seemed genuine. It was nice.

"Yeah. He's the reason I've had any success. I would've kept doing small plays and working on craft. Hank dragged me to movie sets. He was always the one with a vision, the one telling me I would be something."

"A superstar director befriended you and insisted you were talented?" She let out a huff of air. "That's a *way* better story than me becoming an accountant."

He took a step back and eyed her. "Maybe to the casual observer."

She tilted her head. "What's that supposed to mean?"

Russell nodded toward her Mazzy Star shirt. "Well, for one, you're too punk rock to be boring."

Sheila shook her head. "I'm not punk anymore. I'm a middle-aged mom. I went back to the grocery store last month because I realized I hadn't paid for my paper towels on self-checkout and the guilt was killing me."

"I don't buy it. You were in a band!"

She narrowed her eyes. "Did Eliza tell you that?"

"No. I can just tell." Not entirely true. Eliza had mentioned it, in a more, "Can you believe my mom was in a band?" type of way.

He thought it made perfect sense.

Sheila laughed. "Fine. Yes, I was in a band, but becoming an accountant was my first choice. I love music, but I needed something stable."

Ah, finally. Some truth. "Was it because you didn't want to disappoint your parents? Because let me tell you, mine were not happy when I told them I was becoming an actor."

"Eh...not exactly." She wiped her hands on a rag, her eyes cast upward, pensive. "My mom was...eccentric. She wasn't around much, and my dad always struggled with money. I promised myself I'd have a stable career and never have to worry like he did. I didn't want to rebel. I wanted to...I don't know. Excel?"

"That was smart."

"Yeah, ha. Except that didn't work out either. I met my husband in the band. Did you know divorce is one of the leading causes of bankruptcy?"

Oh, he knew. He thought he might be nearing it himself, but he'd let her discover that on her own.

"Is it?"

Her eyes glanced at him, then flitted away. "Yeah. I'm not bankrupt, I'm just...believe me, I'm very good with money."

"I'm sure you are."

"Still, there was a time when I was young and dumb. Out of school, I got a job as an accountant at a record studio."

"What?" He did a double take. "Your story is already more interesting than mine. I feel like my life just happened to me, but you had a vision."

"It wasn't a vision." She rolled her eyes, but a smile crept onto her lips. "Did you ever see *Desert Rose Revolution?*"

"Yeah! I loved that movie."

"Do you remember the song 'Grunge and Glitter'?" She bit her lip. "That was me. That was my song."

"You're kidding! That was a great song. *Is* a great song, I mean."

She shrugged. "Yeah, it was fun. I had to leave that behind, though."

"Why? What happened?"

She waved a hand and turned back to the trim. "Eh, you know."

Russell did not know, though he desperately wanted to.

"Do you still write music?"

She poured a small blob of white paint into the tray and gave a non-committal shrug. "Not really."

A memory hit him and he snapped his fingers. "Sheila Wilde! I remember you! I remember your songs!"

"That was my stage name. Sheila Wilde died a long time ago."

"No, she didn't." His gaze drifted up, his mind grasping at a memory he couldn't quite reach. "You had another song."

She was back to painting, back to avoiding him. "Yeah..."

The words snapped into his memory and he repeated them in his best sing-song voice. "Oh daughter, oh daughter of mine. When did you learn to speak when spoken to? Oh daughter, my darling, so fine. When you're silent there's always a why."

She was looking at him now. "You have a good memory."

"How can you say you're boring when you wrote something like that?"

Eliza popped into the room carrying a tray. "Granny made us all lunch, but she insists she's still too afraid to come in to see the shop until we're done."

She set down the tray – sandwiches, a potato salad, hot tea, and a little flower in a glass.

"Thanks, honey," Sheila said.

"It looks great in here!" Eliza stood with her hands on her hips. "I think we're getting really close."

Sheila's aching, soulful song echoed in Russell's mind. He had to pull himself out of it and stop being weird. "How's the website coming?" he asked.

"It's okay. I spent like nine hours on it yesterday and my eyes are starting to cross. Granny's got a lot of teas here, and getting them online is a pain."

Sheila nodded. "You won't convince her to change it, so don't even try."

"I won't. I'm actually thinking we should set up an online shop to sell them. It'll take more time, though."

"I think that's a wonderful idea!" Sheila said.

Eliza nodded. "Should we eat outside? This paint smell is making me dizzy. I found the cushions for the chairs."

"Sure," Sheila said. "Is that okay with you, Russ?"

"Fine by me." He smiled. Only his friends called him Russ. He liked the idea of Sheila becoming his friend.

Or maybe something more.

He stopped walking. It felt like something had popped in his chest, like a pilot light coming to life. He could feel his heartbeat quickening and his chest growing warmer under the bright blue flame.

"I'll be out in a minute," he said, walking toward the bathroom.

He needed a moment to himself to process that thought, the literal spark he'd just felt.

Inside the small, poorly lit bathroom, he locked the door. Patty had decorated this to look like the inside of a red telephone booth. There was a picture of Big Ben on one wall and a tiny version of the London Eye collecting dust near the sink.

Russell braced himself on the edge of the sink and tried to understand what had just happened, taking a few deep breaths and looking at himself in the mirror.

Sheila's comment about him deciding he was good-looking flashed in his mind, and he smiled.

His chest was still burning. He hadn't felt anything like this in years. For so long, he'd been happily married, and the idea of being attracted to anyone else seemed so foreign, so impossible...

This was new territory. Somewhere he never thought he'd be.

He turned the water on. At first it was a few drops, then it turned into more of spray.

Something else to look into fixing.

The water was cold, at least, and he splashed it onto his face. There was no need to rush this feeling, no need to spook whatever this spark was. No need to question it out of existence.

For now, it was enough to know he could feel something again. He dried his face and walked outside to join them.

Eighteen

I t was easy to forget Russell's stardom when he was in a ratty t-shirt scrubbing floorboards or painting walls. Now, watching him walk out of the tea shop in his black bomber jacket and aviator sunglasses, he looked very much like the celebrity he was and Sheila felt exposed.

Overexposed, actually. Why had she babbled so much? He didn't want to hear her life story. He was just being polite. Or maybe he was researching a new role, learning to play a boring accountant, and that's why he was spending time with an old widow and her progeny.

Thankfully, Eliza had about a hundred questions for Russell, so Sheila could sit back and be quiet. He'd played a rather convincing spy in the movie *Tactical Deception,* and he wasn't shy about discussing it.

"They had me spend time with a spy," Russell told them. "For two weeks, I lived with the guy."

Eliza shot back in her seat. "How did they find a spy? Was that even safe?"

"I have no idea, and sure. It was as safe as can be. I mean, I feel like the guy had killed people. But he didn't have any orders to kill me." He flashed a smile. "Though maybe he wanted to kill me by the end."

"Who did he kill?"

"I didn't ask. He didn't talk much. It was a strange two weeks. I just tried to watch him. He always checked exits wherever we went. Now I do the same thing. It's about the only thing I learned from him."

Sheila smiled but kept her thoughts to herself. She'd done enough sharing for the day and, after lunch, she excused herself back to the cottage.

There was work to be done there, too. First, she answered emails from her newly poached accounting clients. A few had followed her as soon as they heard she'd left the firm, and others had agreed to work with her once she emailed them personally. Her old boss would be furious, but then, he shouldn't have fired her.

After that was done, she faced the pile of papers Patty had dug up about the tea shop's insurance.

It had taken Patty much longer to compile the paperwork than it took Sheila to go through it. There was nothing there about liquidating the tea shop. Sheila had no idea where Patty had gotten that idea.

There were some business documents they needed, and Sheila scanned them and sent them to the insurance agent. Hopefully they'd be officially covered by next week.

The next issue was Sheila's house back in Lynnwood. The bank had called and left a message warning that if she missed one more payment, they would be forced to start the foreclosure process.

What did that really mean, though? If the process was just starting, she had time to make money, right?

Eliza was so against renting the house out that she hadn't wanted to broach the topic again, but she might have to. The accounting clients she'd taken on wouldn't pay her until the end of the next quarter. She knew she needed to put in effort to find new clients, but there never seemed to be enough time in the day. Between renovating the tea shop, taking over Patty's grocery shopping, cleaning, and laundry, then fielding Patty's complaints about losing said chores, Sheila fell into bed every day exhausted.

She sat back and closed her eyes. It would be so nice to just take a little nap...

But no. She couldn't. She needed to figure out her expenses. She needed to get on top of the mortgage. How many more clients did she need? Did she need to find a new job right away, or could it wait a few months?

A familiar dread filled her stomach. No wonder Patty refused to go into the tea shop. It wasn't that she couldn't face the dust or the burnt-out lights. She couldn't face the shame.

Sheila knew it well. As brilliant an accountant as she was, she couldn't look at her own bank account or her own credit cards.

They weren't just numbers. They were memories and regrets, a knee-deep mud she got stuck in every time she overdrew her checking account.

Tomorrow. She could face it tomorrow.

She shut her laptop and got up to switch the laundry.

. . .

That weekend, Sheila hardly saw Eliza. She was holed up in the cottage, creating an online shop and adding a new online payment system. She only came down briefly when something smelled irresistible and, on Saturday, it was Patty's mascarpone french toast.

"The online payments are going to make it much easier for young people to come to the tea shop, which is what you want."

"You mean children?" Patty asked with complete sincerity.

"Uh, sort of. I mean everyone. You can't run a cash-only business in this day and age."

Patty frowned, then turned to fill her baking dish with soap and hot water. "Reggie's been telling me the same thing. I guess he was right."

Sheila took her last bite of french toast and cleared her plate. "I'm going into town to meet with Inge if you'd like to join."

"Is that the lady who's going to fix the shutters?" Patty asked.

"No, she's the orca researcher. I'm going to talk to her about Lottie and play the recording for her."

She'd wanted to meet with her right away, but Inge had been in the Arctic, collecting data on whale populations, until last night.

Patty clapped her hands together. "I'd love to! Let me grab my purse."

They met at a bakery in town. It was busy, as good bakeries tend to be, crowded with good foods and good smells. Inge was already in line and Sheila and Patty stood behind her.

Sheila got a coffee and everyone else got tea. They took a seat at a table near a window to share an assortment of pastries.

"Don't ask me how I got this," Sheila said, sliding her phone across the table. "But this is a recording of Lottie vocalizing."

Inge looked up from her tea, intrigued. She hit play and Lottie's song rang out, melancholy and sweet.

Inge listened intently, and when the recording was through, she looked up, her eyes round and bright. "You were right. She's a resident orca! I'm sure of it. I can't believe this."

"You know that just from a recording?" asked Patty.

Inge nodded, speaking quickly. "Oh yes. It's very easy to tell them apart from their calls. They all have different dialects, and her calls are just like the rest of the L-pod whales."

"That's remarkable!" Patty said. "Whom do we need to talk to, to get her released?"

Inge sat back and sighed. "If only it were that easy."

Sheila's heart sank. "I thought if I could prove she was a resident orca, they would have to release her. Aren't they considered endangered?"

Inge nodded slowly, her gray eyes sharp and focused. "It helps, of course, to know Lottie is the last resident orca in captivity. It's like a second chance to make things right after what happened with Tokitae."

"The Florida whale?" Patty asked.

Inge bit her lip. Her eyes shone with tears, and she blinked them away. "Yes. We were almost ready to build a sea pen and pull together a team of veterinarians and behaviorists to welcome her back into her home waters. But then she passed away. It just took us too long and..." Her voice trailed off. She took a sip of tea before speaking again. "The fact that there's another resident orca...? It's a miracle, honestly. We could help her. We really could."

Her passion was contagious. Sheila hadn't had any of her coffee, nor a single bite of food. The way Inge spoke about whales reminded her of Russell and his wolves.

Sheila wasn't whale-crazy, and she definitely wasn't wolf-crazy. But she was crazy about Lottie. "Is there a chance her mom is still alive?"

Inge nodded. "Can I see the pictures?"

"Sure." Sheila reached into her purse and pulled out the old, grainy Polaroids she had taken in the cove. "I'm not sure if you can tell from these pictures, but there's Lottie, and her mom is back there."

Inge picked up one of the pictures, squinting. "I can't believe this. Do you see that mark of black on her saddle patch?"

Sheila didn't, but she said, "Yes."

"They nicknamed her Streak because of that marking. She's still alive! She just swam by the Lime Kiln lighthouse last week."

"That's incredible!" Sheila leaned in, more determined to see the streak she was talking about.

Patty tutted. "I don't know about this. What if Lottie can't make it? What if she starves to death?"

Inge shot forward and almost spilled her tea. "No, no, we would *never* release her into the wild to fend for herself. She'd live in the sea pen, and we'd still monitor her and feed her. She could still hunt, if she wanted to, and we would take her for daily swims following a boat. It would be more like retirement for her. She wouldn't have to perform anymore."

"Would her family – her pod – be able to see her? Hear her?" Sheila asked.

Inge was grinning now, still marveling over the pictures in her hands. "Oh yes, of course! It would be quite a reunion."

"Do you think Streak would recognize her?" Patty asked.

Inge set the pictures down. "Would you recognize your child after not seeing them for forty years?"

Patty sat back, clutching her tea in both hands. "Of course I would!"

"It sounds perfect." Sheila thrust her phone forward again. "Can you take the recording, then? Tell everyone she belongs here and deserves to come home."

Inge reached for the phone, but quickly pulled her hand back. "I can only guess how you got that recording. The owners of Marine Magic Funland would sue me into the ground if I came forward with it, saying I broke into the stadium."

"Oh." Sheila frowned. She couldn't afford a lawsuit now, either. "Can I release it anonymously?"

Inge thought on it. "Possibly. Then me and a few other researchers could confirm the validity of Lottie's calls." She paused. "The pictures you have would help, too, but without your story behind it, they would claim they're fake."

This wasn't what she was hoping to hear. Sheila felt like she'd done her part. "What am I supposed to do, then?"

"I think your best bet would be to approach the owners of the park first. See if they'd consider releasing her."

She raised an eyebrow. "Would they?"

"Probably not, but then you can threaten to go public. Tell them the bad publicity will ruin them."

"I was hoping to keep this anonymous," Sheila said.

"I understand, but I don't think you can. It's too easy for them to dismiss an anonymous source, or even anything coming from us. They would claim we fabricated all the evidence. You, however, have no reason to lie."

Patty turned to her, her forehead creased, but said nothing.

It was not the outcome Sheila had hoped for. She thought it would be easy after she proved where Lottie had come from. Threatening the owners of Marine Magic Funland had not been in her plans.

"Thanks for your help," she said. "I have a lot to think about."

On the drive home, Patty talked about the rain, the fog that morning, and about needing to clean the windows in the kitchen.

It took her nine minutes to break down. "Oh, just give it to me! I'll say I was the one who saw her captured and that I was the one who broke into the whale stadium to get the recording. Who's going to arrest a grandma?"

It was a sweet gesture, but Sheila couldn't let it happen. "I'm not going to let you go down for this. It's my responsibility. I need to be the one to do it."

Patty sighed. "I understand."

The phone rang and Sheila's heart jumped. Were they onto her? Did Inge already tell all her friends the good news and now people were going to start asking questions?

Sheila cleared her throat. "Hello?"

"Hey Sheila, it's Russell. How's it going?"

She'd answered the call on speakerphone, but the excited look on Patty's face made her regret it. "Everything's good. How're you?"

"I'm good, I'm good. I, uh – there's this restaurant on the island. Il Palazzo Friday Harbor. Have you heard of it?"

"I haven't, no."

"They have a yacht where they do this seven-course dinner every few months, and I've always wanted to go but felt too embarrassed to go by myself. There's one tomorrow night. I wanted to know if you're busy?"

Patty shot her a look and loudly whispered, "He's asking you on a date!"

Sheila wrestled with her phone, getting it off speaker and quickly pulling it to her ear. "Tomorrow?"

"Feel free to say no. It's just...I can't resist a seven-course Italian dinner. Do you like Italian food?"

Patty jabbed her in the ribs a little too hard. "Say yes!" she whispered.

Sheila shot her an annoyed look. "I do."

"My treat, of course. You can see first-hand how bad I am with money before you really dive into the details."

Patty cut in, yelling, "What time should I send her over?"

They'd reached the cottage, so Sheila parked the car and shut her eyes. This was too much all at once, and she needed to end this call so Patty couldn't say any more. "Sure, yeah. I was meaning to start on your account this week anyway."

"Perfect! I'll tell you more over dinner. Pick you up at six?"

Her heart leapt. Pick her up? This did feel like a date. "See you then."

She hung up. Patty sat in the passenger seat, her hands clasped in her lap, a smile on her face.

"He's no Idris Elba, but you could do worse," she said.

Sheila laughed. "It's just dinner."

"Of course it is."

"We're going to discuss him becoming a client of mine."

Patty laughed. "I bet you are!"

Sheila sighed. There was no winning with her. "I'll see you inside."

Nineteen

It was windy and the ocean was agitated, with white caps in the distance and waves crashing onto shore. Rain poured down, outlining the tea shop in gloom. Not ideal for a boating dinner, but a perfect excuse for Russell to drive one house over to pick Sheila up.

He'd heard Eliza and Sheila say they were going to paint the exterior of both the cottage and the tea shop themselves, and while he agreed it needed to be done, he didn't want them to have to suffer through it. Between scraping the old paint and putting on multiple coats, it could take them a week or more to do it on their own.

He'd wanted to approach Patty about gifting something to the tea shop, joking it would help his own property value, but he knew she'd say no.

His mind was made up. He pulled his phone out of his pocket and made a call.

"Hey. It's Russell Westwood."

"Russell! How's it going? I hope my work is holding up."

"Absolutely. It's great." He leaned forward and narrowed his eyes. It looked like one of the gutters had collapsed in the downpour. That wasn't good. "I'm sure you're booked up for the year, but I've got a job for you when you've got some time."

"I just had a cancellation this week. What's up?"

Russell told him what would need to be done – painting, redoing the roof, and shoring up the gutters. "Don't be surprised if the homeowner comes out to yell at you, then afterwards brings you a plate of cookies."

He chuckled. "Got it. My kind of client. My team will come out on Tuesday. Should be no problem."

Russell ended the call and smiled to himself. Patty would yell at him, but she'd get over it quickly enough.

Sheila was the wildcard. He never knew what she was going to do or say. It was a thrill just to be near her.

He pulled up to the cottage and walked to the door with his umbrella deployed.

Russell didn't know what the rules of dating were anymore – he didn't even know if this was considered a date – but he wanted to make sure Sheila didn't get soaked on her way to the car.

He knocked and, immediately, Derby barked and announced his arrival.

The door opened. "Hey. Sorry. Just one second," Sheila said, holding up a finger.

She wasn't in her normal band t-shirt and jeans, but instead a white shirt with lace at the edges of the neck and a black skirt that hit high on her waist. Her dark hair was straightened and swooped to one side.

His heart thundered in his chest and his mouth hung open. Maybe he wasn't ready to go out with anyone. Maybe he needed a few more years with the wolves...

"No problem," he managed to say before kneeling to pet Derby.

Sheila disappeared and returned a moment later with her purse on her shoulder.

"You kids have fun!" Patty yelled as she shuffled into view. "Don't stay out too late or you're grounded, Sheila! No ice cream!"

Sheila kept her eyes facing forward. "Good night, Patty." She stepped outside and shut the door firmly behind her. "No one ever warns you about that."

He held the umbrella high to ensure she was covered. "About what?"

"About living with your ex-mother-in-law."

A laugh burst out of him. "You're right. People talk all the time about how moving in with your ex-mother-in-law is easy and trouble-free. They never talk about how they hog all the ice cream."

"Exactly. Liars, every one of them."

The dock was a fifteen-minute drive and Russell was excited to share the playlist he'd put together. "It's not quite as good as one of yours," he said as they settled into their seats, "but I added some of my favorites."

She scrolled through the list on his phone with a half-smile on her face. "The Cranberries, that's good. Nirvana, very cool. Didn't take you for a grunge guy. Sheila Wilde?" She shot a look at him. "A favorite of yours?"

He kept his eyes on the road. "One of the best, yes."

"Oh, this is timely." Sheila tapped a finger and "Only Happy When It Rains" started to play. "I do love the rain."

Russell stole a glance at her. Her head was tilted ever so slightly, looking through the window. "Yeah?"

"I love the sound. The rain fills all the empty spaces. It makes the world seem smaller and wipes it all clean."

The rain was the one thing he was still getting used to. It had been a glorious summer, dry and sunny, but now every day had rain forecasted for at least part of the day. He never knew when to trust a rainy forecast. "I need to learn to embrace it."

They got to the dock, and as soon as he parked, Russell got out and ran over to her side of the car with the umbrella.

"It's okay," she said, waving him off. "I feel bad. We don't both fit under there."

"I'm fine."

"But you don't have your hat," she continued. "Your hair's going to get wet."

He held the umbrella over her. "I wear the hat more as a disguise."

"Your hair's real? I thought it was a toupee. Or...what is it you stars do? Hair transplants?"

He laughed so hard he started coughing. "My hair is real and non-transplanted. Thank you for the backhanded compliment."

She grinned as they walked down the dock and onto the waiting ship.

Russell had never been a ship person, but even he was impressed. It was pristine, all white, with clean lines and the warm glow of lights in the night.

They stepped on board and were rushed into the cozily lit cabin. Russell was pleased to see Sheila had remained dry. He ran a hand through his hair, shaking off the raindrops, and caught the eye of the hostess.

"Hi there, two for –"

"You're…" She stared at him, pointing, her eyes round with wonder.

He knew that look. She was either sifting through her memory, trying to place his face, or she was too awestruck to speak. "Russell. Nice to meet you."

"I am a huge fan! I loved you in *Pictures of a Perfect Marriage.*"

It was always flattering when someone told him they'd enjoyed one of his movies, always pleasantly surprising that anyone would take the time to watch something he'd done.

With that movie, though, he'd played a terrible person – and a terrible husband – and while he didn't regret it, it sometimes made him wonder what people thought of him.

Did they think he was like that in real life? That his marriage was filled with him bellowing abuse behind closed doors and showing smiles to the rest of the world?

"It's so nice to meet you," she added, extending a handshake. "That movie reminded me so much of my dad. I've never seen anything depicted on screen that was so…realistic. I could tell people, '*That* was what my dad was like.' It felt like no one understood."

He took her hand, cupping it with both of his. "Well. I'm sorry to hear that..." He peeked at her name tag. "Carla. I hope the movie wasn't too hard to watch."

"With you? Never!" She sucked in a breath, smiling widely. "Can I get a picture? My mom will *die* when she sees it."

"Of course."

He stepped to her side and she extended her arm in front of them.

"Do you want me to take it?" Sheila asked.

"Yes!" Carla handed the phone over and ran her hands over her hair, then dropped her arms to her sides. "Ah, I don't know what to do with my hands!"

Sheila pointed. "Give him bunny ears." She paused. "Smile. Perfect."

"Thank you so much!" Carla said, rushing forward. "I can't believe this!"

"Tell your mom he's wearing a toupee," Sheila added.

Carla zoomed in on a picture. "Wait, really?"

Russell covered his eyes with his hand. "Now if I deny it, I look like I've got something to hide."

"I'm just kidding," Sheila said. "He has great hair."

"Really great hair!" Carla agreed, beaming. She put her phone back into her pocket and picked up two menus. "I'm so sorry. You probably want to sit down. Follow me!"

They wove through the little restaurant to a small, round table topped with a white tablecloth and a single white candlestick.

They took their seats and Sheila asked, "Does that happen everywhere you go?"

Russell shrugged. "It depends. The beard helps people not recognize me. The hat helps more. What helps most of all is not doing any more movies so people forget I exist."

Sheila picked up the wine list and held it in her hand. "Don't you miss it? Making movies?"

He stared at the menu in front of him. They were going to start with canederli, then a braised carrot salad, then a truffle risotto. The main dish was a Chianti-braised beef with polenta and gremolata, and dessert was a white wine cheesecake.

"It's complicated," he finally said.

Sheila was watching him with those pretty gray eyes. Her eyeshadow had a touch of sparkle, and it caught in the low light.

He looked back down. He wasn't supposed to ogle his non-date.

"Is that topic off-limits?" she asked gently. "Like your toupee?"

He cracked a smile. "This might sound dramatic, but sometimes it feels like nothing good came out of me doing movies."

"What do you mean? You mean the fame?"

He shook his head, trying to figure out what he wanted to say. "I've never been particularly comfortable with that part, but no." He sighed. "When I met Holly, we were both just starting out, and then all of a sudden my career took off. It was just a few movies, and all because of Hank. Nothing really to do with me."

Sheila narrowed her eyes and leaned in. "You have to give yourself *some* credit."

"It's not fair, the actor's life." He shrugged. "Holly was really talented, but she wasn't getting any roles. She had to watch everyone fawn over me. Every time I dragged her to a premiere or an award show, I could feel her slipping away. Withdrawing into herself, growing more self-conscious. It was stupid, it was destructive, and I didn't want anything to do with it."

The waitress stopped by to get their drink orders. Sheila was still holding the wine list.

"Do you want to pick a bottle of wine?" Russell asked.

Sheila shook her head and dropped her voice. "They're a little pricey."

"We have a wine pairing," the waitress said. "Each course comes with a glass of wine chosen by Chef."

"Chosen by Chef," Russell repeated. "I don't think we can top that."

"I can come back," the waitress offered, her eyes lingering on Russell.

He nodded. "Thank you."

"That's too much," Sheila said, shifting in her seat. "I'll stick with water."

"Do you like wine?" Russell asked.

"Of course I like wine, but –"

He looked at her and said nothing.

"It's too much," Sheila whispered. "They're taking you for a ride because you're a celebrity."

Russell laughed and set the menu down. "It's okay. I'm used to it."

She smiled, the mischief returning to her eyes. "Everybody wants something from you, don't they?"

"Yes." He paused. He wanted to add *Everyone but you*, but he couldn't bring himself to say the words. Instead, he caught the waitress' eye and told her they'd like to have all the recommended wine pairings.

"So much for a little bit of wine..." Sheila shook her head. "You really are bad with money."

"You're looking at it the wrong way," he said with a grin. "I'm good at *spending* money."

Sheila set her menu down. "Was Holly jealous, then? Of your success?"

"No. She wasn't jealous. It was worse than that." He took a deep breath. "It made her sad, and that broke my heart. Looking back...man. I wasn't even that big back then. We were able to move to Minneapolis and live normal lives. Almost normal, whatever that is. She was the one who suggested it – she wanted a break from trying to get into the business, and then we had Lucas. We were close to my parents; it was great. This business..."

He looked around. It was best if no one was close enough to overhear what he was saying. Thankfully, they weren't. "I don't want to say anything bad about the people in it, because a lot of them are my friends. But make no mistake, it's a rat race like anywhere else. It's competitive. There's a lot of money involved. People get crazy about money."

"That I know well," Sheila said.

"After a few years, people started forgetting who I was. It was wonderful. Then we had Mia and we were happy. At least, I thought we were."

She stared at him, her eyes calm, her expression neutral.

Russell cleared his throat. "I'm sorry. You don't want to hear about this."

"Please!" She waved a hand. "I've already used you for my divorce support group. I'm happy to return the favor."

He leaned forward, resting his arms on the table. "When the kids moved out, I thought we could start traveling or open a little business. She always wanted to have a flower shop." In some parallel universe, he was cutting roses and making bouquets. He smiled at the thought. "Then Hank came to me with the script. *Pictures of a Perfect Marriage*. He wanted us to play husband and wife. Said it'd be a comeback. Holly begged me to do it, so we did."

Sheila winced. "I'm embarrassed to say I haven't seen it. I heard it was about a bad marriage and...yeah. Couldn't stomach it for some reason."

Russell smiled. "No offense taken. It was really Holly's movie. She shined. She won an Oscar, and the offers started rolling in. She was so happy, and I was happy for her."

"But then..." Sheila said, raising and eyebrow.

He nodded. "But then."

Sheila clasped her hands together dramatically. "That was when she told you she was running away with the pool boy?"

If only.

He couldn't tell her the truth. No one knew why Holly had left him. People assumed he was a terrible husband, like in the movie.

That was easier than the truth, less painful than the fact that during the entire production of the movie, she and Hank were falling in love.

He cleared his throat. "She just didn't want the life we'd planned together anymore."

He fell silent, the sound of the other diners filling the space between them. They stared at each other for a moment in the candlelight.

Then she spoke. "I guess that's what all divorces are. 'You know that future we planned together? I don't want that anymore.'"

"Yeah. Exactly." Their first glasses of wine arrived and he took a sip. It was dry and heavy. "Life is full of surprises, though. I've made peace with it."

There were other surprises, too. Like sitting at a table across from a clever, irreverent woman. A woman who made him laugh, who made him think there was a chance at joy, whose eyes looked so beautiful in the candlelight.

"It's brutal, isn't it?" she asked.

He couldn't take his eyes off her. "Yeah. Brutal."

Twenty

There was something dreamlike about sitting there with him, the rain pattering on the ship's windows, the candlelight flickering between them. The food was heavenly, every course that arrived more delicious than the last, and the tension she carried in her shoulders softened and disappeared.

Sheila sat back with a glass of red wine in her hand. Maybe it wasn't a dream, but a scene from someone else's life. Someone who hadn't gotten fired, someone who wasn't facing foreclosure on their home. Someone who wasn't full of mistakes.

Surely it had to be Russell's life and she was merely an extra, even less significant than the people staring at him and sneaking pictures from behind.

Her nerves fizzled out, softened by the rain and swept away by his laugh. Russell had a great laugh, deep and rolling, like the sound of an engine purring to life.

She liked getting him to laugh. It egged her on and kept her talking, even when she should, perhaps, keep quiet.

"What about your ex-husband?" he asked. "Was he jealous of your success?"

This wine really was better than the cheap stuff she normally bought. She took a sip and savored the hint of black currant. "What success?"

"Your songs. You met in a band, right? I assumed he was musical too."

Sheila put her wine glass on the table and set her expression flat. "Brian was *never* jealous. It was just that me doing a recording session was inconvenient for his work schedule. And I practiced too loudly for him to concentrate, so I had to do it outside, or, better yet, not at all. When I was invited to play the opening act for a band for three nights, he rightly pointed out that I was abandoning the family."

A smile flickered onto Russell's face. "They'd surely starve to death before your return."

He'd picked up on her sarcasm, which was good, because she was laying it on thick. "I found out a few months ago that he told one of our old friends I'm the reason we got divorced."

Creases formed on Russell's forehead. "Yeah? What reason was that?"

Sheila knew she shouldn't, but she couldn't stop herself. "He said I put my delusions of wanting to be a rock star over my responsibilities as a mother and wife."

He raised an eyebrow and, before he could say anything, she heard herself speaking again. "It's pathetic, what actually happened."

"Maybe him," he said softly. "Not you."

Two slices of white wine cheesecake drizzled with blueberry syrup arrived. Sheila was stuffed, but she wasn't going to stop now. She picked up her fork and took a bite.

"You know how in movies," she said, her mouth full, "when a wife finds out her husband's cheating, she yells at him and throws all his stuff out the window? Or beats up his truck with a bat?"

He nodded.

"I didn't do any of that. I don't know what's wrong with me, but after I accidentally found the email, the one from *her*, I didn't say anything. Not about the affair.

"I said we should go to couple's counseling, and then when we were there, I said I would turn down whatever invitations I'd gotten for my music, that I wouldn't play any openers or ever go on tour. I said I wouldn't write songs anymore, and I meant it." She took another bite of cheesecake, this time chewing before she spoke again. "I gave into his complaints. I promised to make myself smaller and smaller, as out of the way as he needed me to be just so he wouldn't leave."

Russell hadn't touched his cheesecake. He didn't drink his wine or his water. He sat with an elbow on the table and his head resting on his hand, staring at her.

"It was never enough," she said, digging her fork furiously into the cheesecake and shoving a huge bite into her mouth. "After one of our counseling sessions, he told me he wanted a divorce. Before our divorce was final, he'd moved to New York City."

"To be with her?"

Sheila nodded, scraping the last bits of syrup from her plate. "He moved in with her and her two kids. Told our girls to not forget to write. Eliza and Mackenzie were in college then. Shelby was seventeen. Emma was thirteen."

Russell rubbed his face with his hands. "I'm sorry, Sheila."

She didn't need his pity. She didn't know what she needed, but it wasn't that. "No, I'm sorry," she rushed to add. "I don't want to sound bitter. I'm *not* bitter. I'm just...processing. I thought time healed all wounds, but in this case, it hasn't."

Not only had she eaten a slice of cheesecake in front of him like an animal, she'd also unloaded this onto him as though she didn't have friends who heard it a dozen times, as though it had just happened.

Sheila sat back, her cheeks growing hot.

He rubbed his chin and added in a soft voice, "I don't know how we make peace with betrayal, and not just the cheating. He was supposed to believe in you. Support you."

"I could've dealt with him being angry about my music, honestly. I was desperate to make things work, but not for myself. I was desperate for our family." She shook her head and let out a huff. "I am still *so angry* at him for my girls. They deserve better than the father he's become. I don't think I'll ever make peace with that."

Russell was quiet, studying her. His eyes locked onto hers. "You won't be sad forever."

Her eyes flashed with tears and she had to look away – down at her empty plate, out through the window. She picked up her water and took a sip. The feeling passed.

She nodded toward his cheesecake. "Are you going to eat that or what?"

Twenty-one

That. That was it. The moment his heart was irrevocably gone.

"I'm just kidding," she said with a laugh.

He pushed the plate toward her. "Please. It's yours."

Whatever she wanted. It was hers.

Twenty-two

The next morning, Patty didn't torture her too much about her evening out.

"You had a nice time, then?" she asked, her eyes and hands busy with the pepperoni rolls she was making for lunch.

Though Sheila had hoped Patty would slow down now that she didn't have to do all the chores on her own, it only emboldened her to cook and bake more. Reggie tried to keep up, stopping by with various roasts and creations he'd made, but he had no chance with Patty. She'd become a machine.

"It was very nice, yes," Sheila said, slipping into a seat at the kitchen table. "The restaurant was fantastic."

Patty looked up for a brief flash. "We should go sometime."

"I'd love to."

Eliza stopped down and said hello before getting a plate of food and disappearing. She told them she was *this* close to finishing the online shop and she couldn't stop for pleasantries.

Sheila wasn't sure if the novelty of having a celebrity neighbor was wearing off, or if they were both just busy, but she would take it.

She ate the elaborate breakfast Patty prepared, a large Belgian waffle loaded with whipped cream and strawberries, and avoided bringing up anything having to do with Russell.

When he'd dropped her off the night before, he'd asked if she was ready to take him on as a client.

"I have to warn you," he'd said. "I'm one of those terrible people who has papers and folders and accounts everywhere."

"It's nothing I can't handle," she assured him.

At the time, she had still been all warm and relaxed from their night out. She'd felt seen by him, so seen that she'd almost burst into tears.

Now, in the cold light of morning, she was embarrassed by all she'd told him – about her marriage, about how *weak* she'd been. How weak and bitter she still was.

Regardless, she needed the money. Once she was finished with breakfast, she pulled her coat on and slipped outside.

The wind gusted and blustered, blasting her hair and making a mockery of her jacket. Sheila pulled the sides of it tight across her chest as she walked up the hill to Russell's place.

She got some relief from the wind when she entered the thicket of trees between their properties. Russell's house was barely visible, and she used it as a guide through the smattering of pines and Madrona trees. It only took a minute or two for her to emerge on the other side, with Russell's dark two-story home towering over her.

It was smaller than she'd imagined – larger than Patty's cottage for sure, but not the multi-winged mansion she'd expected of a Hollywood star – and the next neighbor's house was in full view, only thirty feet away.

She picked up her pace and peered around the back of the house, the side that faced the ocean. Both floors had wide, open windows reflecting the sun and sea, and there was a stone patio with comfortable-looking furniture and a fire pit. It looked like a nice place to roast marshmallows and look at the sea.

"Hey there."

Sheila jumped. Russell was standing on the back patio dressed in a green and black flannel shirt, a mug in his hand.

"Hi!" She waved. "Sorry, I didn't mean to creep around. I just wove through the little forest and popped out here."

"I know what you're doing." He narrowed his eyes. "You're sizing me up as a client. Seeing how far of a ride you can take me on."

She shrugged. "Guilty."

"The joke's on you. I'm going to tell you all my financial secrets anyway." He smiled. "Do you want a cup of coffee?"

The wind picked up and she dug her hands into her pockets. "Sure."

Sheila carefully made her way down the rocky bluff and followed Russell inside, closing the doors behind her and shutting out the wind. Inside, she breathed in the warmth, the smell of coffee and fresh bread filling the air.

"These just came out of the oven ten minutes ago." He waved a hand over the baking tray on the kitchen island lined with buttery croissants. "Full disclosure: I bought them frozen. So they'd be, you know, good. Unlike if I tried to make them."

As tempting as they smelled, Sheila declined. "Patty doesn't let me leave the house until I consume at least a thousand calories. I'm still full, but thank you."

The kitchen and living room were one large, open space, with the couch facing the windows and a large kitchen island behind it. The cabinets were rich, stained wood with copper pulls, and the countertop was glossy butcher block.

"Your house is beautiful," she said, running her hand over the kitchen island.

"Thank you. I did a lot to it before I moved in. Not me, I mean – you've seen my work – but a company I hired. They're good. They could help at the cottage."

He poured coffee into a white and terracotta mug and handed it to her.

She accepted it, glad to warm her hands. "Yeah. Maybe."

"It's a shame I couldn't do more myself." He stood with his hands on his hips, looking around. "I thought I would learn woodworking at some point. Spontaneously, you know? Like it would come along with the beard."

Sheila let out a *tsk*. "I hate it when beards don't live up to the special powers they promised."

"Me too."

The wall nearest to her was covered in pictures. She walked over, expecting to see Russell with his celebrity friends, or hundreds of shots of wolves, but instead there were pictures of a boy and a girl playing in the snow, then at the beach, then standing, arms crossed, with Big Ben behind them.

"Is this Lucas and Mia?" she asked.

He stepped up next to her. "Yeah. Mia told me I was ruining her decorating by putting up these pictures, but I love them."

"Is she an interior decorator?" Sheila looked around again, her eyes lingering on all the little details – the red rug, the ombre fuzzy blanket casually draped over the couch.

He shook his head. "No, but she's very good. She chose the furniture, the paint, the design of the beams here." He pointed at the wooden beams above their heads. "This was all her. I just paid."

"She did an excellent job."

"I agree. But again, I feel that you're really not understanding how bad I am with money. I handed my credit card to my twenty-three-year-old daughter."

Sheila laughed. If only he knew how bad she was with money. "I guess I'm finally going to find out."

He grinned. "My office is upstairs. I think I managed to gather all my papers. Might be missing some assets. I'm not sure."

Missing some assets? What a rich person problem. "Let's check it out."

He led the way up the stairs and Sheila followed. She couldn't help but admire him – his broad shoulders, the muscles of his arms underneath his flannel shirt. His neck...

What would it be like to kiss Russell Westwood's neck?

No, she wasn't here for that! He wanted her to do his taxes. To help them with his budget. *Not* kiss his neck. He didn't ask for that, and it would be bizarre for her to try.

Though it was a beautiful neck...

"I apologize for the mess," he said, opening the door to the left of the stairs. "It's not a room I use much, so I end up abandoning a lot of things in there and closing the door."

"I understand," she said with a laugh. "I do that to my finances, too."

They walked in and Sheila ran a hand over the desk. It was covered in papers, piled on either side and scattered across the middle. A large computer screen sat in the center, dust collecting along the back. The wolf pictures were sequestered here, apparently, and the walls were covered with them.

"This is it." He picked up a brown paper bag and handed it to her. "I'm really sorry it's so messy. My last accountant told me I was a nightmare, but I still haven't been able to change my ways."

Sheila laughed and peered inside the bag. "That's a lot of papers. Are you running a business from here or something?"

"No. People just send me everything in the mail and I throw it in the bag. Sometimes I don't even open the envelopes." He winced, rubbing the back of his neck. "Again, I will pay you fairly. I know what a mess this is."

"I have to warn you, I bill by the hour, and my rate goes up on the island. Difficulty getting supplies and all. You understand."

He smiled. "I do." Russell stepped toward her and pulled a folder out of the bag. "These are my bank statements for the last four years."

A chortled laugh escaped from her. "I don't really need that to do your taxes. It seems like you're really looking for someone to yell at you about how much money you spend."

"Yes, yes, I am. It's honestly embarrassing how much money I've lost. I need to know how quickly I'm burning through my savings. I need a budget."

It seemed like the solution to low cash flow was easy for a big star. She shifted the weight of the bag in her hands. "Worst case scenario, you might have to call up your buddy Hank and do another movie."

He was quiet for a moment. "I can't do that."

"Oh? Is that not how it works?"

"We don't talk." Russell shook his head. "And I'm not doing movies anymore."

Sheila felt her shoulders drop. "Russell. If you really are burning through your savings, you can't just not work anymore."

"I can't hear you," he said with a dramatic sigh. "I'm asking for your help."

"All right, all right!" Sheila laughed. "I'm helping you!"

Budgets were easy, as long as it wasn't her own. She'd do what she could.

He tucked the folder back into the bag. "I'm trusting you, Wilde. You should know I don't trust anyone. Except the wolves."

"Ha, right."

He cleared his throat. "It's been – well, I should've told you last night. I'm just so used to *not* telling people."

She tilted her head. "Not telling people what?"

Russell sighed. "When Holly and I did that movie – that was the end. She and Hank...they got together. I didn't know it at the time, but..."

His voice trailed off and the reality of what he was trying to say hit her, twisting her stomach up into her lungs.

Sheila let out a breath. "Russell. I'm so sorry. He was your best friend, wasn't he?"

"One of them, yeah." He scratched his eyebrow. "It's in the past now. But when I say I trust you, I mean it, and I'm so glad to have met you. Really."

There were moments when she was with him that she could forget who he was and enjoy the moment.

This was not one of those times. He was inches from her face. His sterling gaze, the intoxicating scent of his cologne. The cozy warmth of the house...

He leaned forward, ever so slightly, and she realized he was about to kiss her.

Sheila sucked in a sharp breath and stepped back. "I better get going," she announced a bit too loudly. "I can have this back to you in a few days."

He cleared his throat. "Sure. Of course. Thank you again. I really appreciate it."

Her feet had taken her to the doorway of the office. "I think we're going to show Patty the tea shop tomorrow. Do a big debut. Do you want to stop by?"

He scratched his head. "I wish I could, but I can't."

"Have a good day then!" she said, scooting into the hallway, walking away as fast as her legs could carry her.

Twenty-three

"Are you sure it doesn't sound too threatening?"

Eliza shook her head. "No way, Mom. If anything, it's not threatening enough. You barely make demands. It's more like you're pleading."

Her mom leaned over her shoulder, re-reading the text on the laptop screen. "I just want them to see my side of it. Lottie's side of it."

Eliza knew that was unlikely, but she admired her mom for trying. She always did the right thing, even if it seemed hopeless.

"Let me read over it one more time before you hit send," she said.

Dear owners of Marine Magic Funland,

In the summer of 1982, my father accidentally caught a young orca whale in his fishing net. He kept the little whale in a cove, and I took many pictures of her using my Polaroid camera (please see pictures attached to this email and note the freckle on her chin).

I was nine years old. My favorite band was the Go-Go's, and I named her Lottie, after Charlotte Rafferty.

Lottie was gentle and inquisitive, whistling and clicking at me when I came to visit her. I spent days at the edge of the sea marveling at her, and she spent those days staring back at me. Her mother stayed nearby as well, refusing to leave, crying the most heartbreaking song.

We were not a wealthy family. My father sold Lottie for a small sum and we never spoke of it again.

Lottie's capture has haunted me all my life. Just recently, I discovered she was still alive and living in your park. I also learned Lottie is a member of an endangered group of whales called the southern resident killer whales. They are salmon-eating whales who live in the waters off Seattle and Puget Sound.

No one else knew about Lottie's capture. I spoke to an orca researcher and confirmed the identity of Lottie's mother. It is believed she is still alive.

There is a team of orca researchers, veterinarians, and behaviorists who are ready to retire Lottie into a sea pen. She would be able to swim in her home waters again, and her family will be able to welcome her back.

Please note, I am not a researcher nor associated with the team in any way. I have nothing to gain from Lottie being released, except to clear my conscience. Believe me, it is heavy.

Lottie has faithfully performed for the last four decades. Please consider my request.

Sincerely,
S.

"Are you ready to send it?" Eliza asked.

"Are you *sure* they can't track it?"

Eliza cocked her head to the side. "Do you really think I don't know how to use a VPN and set up a simple burner email?"

Her mom stared at her blankly. "Uh...no?"

"I'm going to hit send."

"Wait! Should we delete the S? Maybe sign it 'Lottie's Old Friend?'"

"Too late." Eliza put her hands up. "It's gone! Off into the world!"

Her mom puffed out her cheeks. "All right. I guess that's that. We'll see what they say. I'm betting they won't even respond."

"Then what are we going to do?"

She frowned. "I don't know yet. Anyway. Should I get Granny up here?"

"Yes!" Eliza closed the burner email and pulled up the tea shop's new website. She couldn't wait to show off all the work she'd done. "We can debut the website first because she'll be less impressed with that, even though it took *way* longer to do. Then we can show her the actual tea shop."

As if on cue, Granny appeared in the doorway. "Who are those men outside?"

Eliza made a face of mock horror. "The Funland people must've tracked us down!"

"You assured me we'd be safe!" Her mom walked to the window and peered through the curtains. "Their truck says Lucky Island Contracting."

Granny threw the window open and stuck her head out. "Excuse me! Excuse me!"

It took a moment for the man who'd just stepped out of the truck to realize where the yelling was coming from. When he spotted Granny in the window, he smiled and waved. "Hello, ma'am. Are you the homeowner?"

"Yes, I am. Who are you?"

"I'm with Lucky Island Contracting." He glanced down at his clipboard. "We're here to redo the paint, siding, and roofs on both existing structures."

"I didn't call anyone," Granny yelled. "If you think you can scam an old lady –"

"Your neighbor hired us. Russell Westwood."

Granny turned around and lowered her voice. "Sheila, did you know about this?"

She shook her head. "He never mentioned it."

Granny turned back to the window. "Well, you can go back to Russell Westwood's house!"

"Sorry, ma'am. I've already been paid, and I'm an honest man. I have to do the work now."

"The nerve of these contractors," she said under her breath.

He went on. "I was warned you'd yell at me. Also, I believe I'm entitled to cookies?"

Granny let out huff. "For heaven's sake. How did Russell know I'm making cookies?"

"Because you're always making cookies," Eliza said. "It's a safe bet." She stuck her head out the window. "Thanks for coming! Please carry on!"

"Eliza!" her mom scolded. "We can't let Russell pay for this. It's inappropriate."

"Hey, if my new stepdad wants to keep me from climbing up a ladder and painting the side of the house, then I say let him." Eliza paused, waiting for her mom to scold her again, but she was silent.

Instead, her eyes were focused on the laptop screen. "Why don't you show Granny what you've been working on?"

Oh. Touchy subject. Eliza bit her lip. She hadn't meant to cause trouble. It seemed like a funny joke after her mom had gone out to dinner with a celebrity.

"Yes, I can't wait to see!" Granny said, leaning in.

Eliza forced a smile. "Okay. So, Granny, I know most of your business is during the summer when there are tourists on the island. I'm hoping to change that." She clicked over to the page that listed each of their 103 teas – the white teas, the black teas, the green and oolong teas. The herbals and pu-erhs. "What I've done is make an online shop where you can sell tea and maybe do some cooking classes for our fans all over the world."

"Do we have fans all over the world?" Granny asked, eyes wide.

"I mean, not yet, but we will," Eliza said. "I've gotten all of the teas onto the website with your descriptions and your pictures."

"Look at that!" Granny said, pointing. "It's wonderful!"

"It's all here: all the information you have about where the tea was grown and how it pairs with food. I've used blog posts to get SEO terms, so anyone searching for tea will arrive on our site, with our expertise and our trusty Granny."

"I don't know what SEO is, but that right there is *me!*" Granny exclaimed when the picture of her came onto screen.

It was from a few years ago, before her hip fracture. She wore a red apron and stood smiling, the sea at her back.

Eliza grinned. "Do you like it?"

"I *love* it." Granny gave her a hug from behind. "This is better than anything I could have imagined."

"I love it, too," her mom said. "Most of all, I love seeing you so excited about something."

Eliza smiled to herself. "Thanks, Mom." She shut her laptop. "Anyway, that's just one part. Are you ready to see your new and improved tea shop?"

Granny clasped her hands together, a wide smile on her face. "I think I am."

They walked outside and Granny briefly stopped to speak to the guy in charge of the construction crew. "I wanted to make sure he was going to match the colors," she said as they walked away. "He said he would. I guess I have no choice but to trust him."

"I can't believe Russell did this," Eliza said as they reached the front door of the tea shop. "I knew he made some jokes about being an investor, but this is a total surprise."

Her mom nodded. "It's very nice of him."

She still wasn't making eye contact. Eliza decided to drop the subject and focus on their debut. "Granny, I present to you: your tea shop!"

She pushed the door open and hurried to turn on the lights.

Granny gasped, her hands covering her mouth. "It's beautiful! It looks brand new!"

"Come on in," Eliza said, taking her gently by the arm. "We upgraded the seating in the lobby – some new cushions to freshen the place up."

"They look wonderful. I love the colors in here."

"That was my choice," Eliza said proudly. "I tidied up the front desk too, so it's easier to make reservations. This tablet will let people pay with credit cards. I'll show you how to use it later. It's really easy."

Granny shot the tablet a distrusting look. "If you say so."

They took Granny through the London room, the Japanese room, and finally the kid's room. They'd polished the little silver bells that sat on each table, the ones patrons would ring when they wanted more tea.

Granny picked one up and rang it. "Music to my ears," she said with a grin.

They ended the tour in the kitchen, where the teacups stood tall and sparkling, ready for the next teatime.

"I was too afraid to come in here and see them all dusty," Granny confessed, picking up a blue-and-gold cup with white flowers. "You've worked magic. Both of you. It looks unbelievable in here. Ray would have loved it. Thank you. Thank you so, so much."

"You're welcome," her mom said, grasping Granny by the hands. "I just have one more call with the insurance agent, and I think we'll get the okay to reopen."

Granny looked around and took a deep breath. "I think you were right. We need to rename it."

"Russell had a good idea," Eliza said. "He thought we should call it 'A Spot of Tea.'"

Granny and her mom looked at each other and smiled.

"What?" Eliza asked. "Not good?"

Her mom shook her head. "No, it's very good. It's perfect. Don't you think so, Patty?"

Granny pulled them both in for a tight hug. "Absolutely perfect."

Twenty-four

Maybe it was time to go back to the wolves. Russell's attempt to rejoin society had been admirable, but he was ready to admit he'd failed.

He kept replaying that moment with Sheila over and over again. He didn't know what had gotten into him. He hadn't planned on trying to kiss her, but they had been in that little office and she was so close...

Maybe his attempted kiss wasn't as obvious as he thought? Maybe it was all in his head?

No. She'd known what he was doing, and she couldn't get out of there fast enough.

The only saving grace was that he'd thought to lie that he couldn't come over for the tea shop debut.

The trouble was he didn't actually have any plans. He decided to leave the island anyway to avoid running into her, and once he was safely on the mainland, he came up with things to do.

His biggest distraction was preparing for Thanksgiving. It was Holly's turn to host the kids, but she was shooting a movie and didn't know if she'd be done in time. Russell wanted to be ready in case the kids decided to come and stay with him.

He set about buying all the little things he was missing – extra pillows, serving dishes. A roasting pan.

That evening, he got dinner with some old friends and, afterward, when he still wasn't quite ready to go back to the island, he booked a hotel room for the night.

Early the next morning, Russell was getting a breakfast sandwich from McDonald's when he got a call from Harry at Marine Magic Funland.

"I'm betting you have great news for me," Russell said.

"No, Russell! I've got bad news!"

Sarcasm didn't translate for Harry. "Aw, really?"

"I know you're a busy man, but I need you to come in. We need to talk. All of us owners."

It was another excuse to stay off-island and he was all for it. "You're in luck. I can be there in an hour or two."

He made the drive over to Marine Magic Funland and approached the front gate slowly. There were roller coasters as far as he could see, whizzing and screaming by.

It wasn't busy, and he wasn't sure if it was normal for it to not be busy, but he suspected so. He'd only been to the park once before, when Holly had been shooting her movie there. He'd come to visit her on set, but she was so annoyed by his presence he didn't dare come again.

Harry was waiting just past the ticket gates. "Come with me. The other owners are here. Have you met them? Mr. and Mrs. Smitt."

"Like the spy movie? Mr. and Mrs. Smith?" Russell asked with a smile.

"They don't like that, don't do that," Harry said, hurrying along.

"What's going on?" Russell asked, following behind. "You're acting like we're under attack."

He looked over his shoulder and lowered his voice. "We are."

They wove through the park and got to a nondescript brown building on the grounds. Inside, Harry led him to a room with a long table.

Mr. and Mrs. Smitt were already there. They were formally dressed and had that long-lived relationship look where they'd started to resemble each other.

Was it the clothes? They both wore gray suit jackets. The husband had a black tie, the wife a black neck scarf.

It was more than that, though. Their faces were the same shape, their eyes the same color, and their skin was the same stage of wrinkling.

Russell had to stop staring. He cleared his throat and introduced himself.

"We know who you are," Mr. Smitt said flatly. "There's no need for theatrics."

"We need him," Mrs. Smitt said under her breath.

Russell took a seat and pretended not to hear them.

"They're coming after us," Harry said, his face red and shiny with sweat. "They're coming for Lottie."

"Who's coming?" asked Russell.

"The crazies. The hippies. Whatever you want to call them." He clicked around the computer sitting on the desk and a projector kicked on. "We got this threatening email yesterday."

Russell read the email as quickly as he could while Harry prattled on.

"This anonymous 'S' claims that Lottie is an endangered species. Can you believe this? They'll say anything so they can have her."

"Our highest earning attraction. Of course they want her," Mrs. Smitt said.

"Or is she our highest-*cost* attraction...?" Mrs. Smitt muttered.

Harry waved a hand and shook his head. "That has nothing to do with it. I love this whale. I've grown up with her. I'd never do anything to harm her."

"Is it true," Russell asked slowly, "that she's one of these endangered whales?"

"Of course not!" Harry bellowed, spit flying from his mouth. "They're making it up. Ever since Tokitae died, all the whale hippies have lost their minds."

"Who's Tokitae?" Russell asked, though the name sounded vaguely familiar.

"She was an orca in Miami. She actually *was* a southern resident whale." Harry shook his head. "Look, it was sad what happened to her. It was. I wish she could've made it back with her family, but Lottie isn't the same. If they try to put her back into the ocean, they're going to kill her. She'll starve to death. The other whales will attack her because she's different."

Russell thought Harry was going to tell him one of the roller coasters had broken down, or that people had gotten food poisoning from the funnel cakes. Not this.

"This is where you come in," Mrs. Smitt said, pointing a long bony finger at him.

"Me?" Russell let out a nervous chuckle. "I'm not sure what I can do."

"You have to protect her," Harry said, his eyes wide. "Please, Russell. We can't lose Lottie. I won't be able to live with myself if she dies. If they go public with this, we're going to need you. We'll need you to be the voice of reason to protect her."

Russell nodded. He didn't want the poor thing to die either. "Don't worry. I'll do whatever you need me to do."

Twenty-five

They didn't hear from Russell for the rest of the week. Sheila assumed he was avoiding her, but she still wasn't sure what had happened, and she wasn't about to talk it out with anyone.

Patty disapproved of his absence and decided to take matters into her own hands. She assumed Russell was avoiding *her*, and she went to his house to thank (and yell at) him for the work on the cottage.

When he wouldn't answer her pounding on the door, she called him and found out he was off island for business. He also asked Patty's advice about hosting a potential Thanksgiving dinner at his new house, which delighted her to no end.

Sheila was mortified. The fact that he'd fled the island was her fault. It had to be.

Maybe he hadn't been trying to kiss her after all? Maybe he'd just stepped close to her and Sheila had jumped away like the deranged woman she was before running out of the house? She'd probably scared the crap out of him and made it unbearably awkward for them both.

She didn't know what had happened, or how he felt, or what he thought. But the worst part was not knowing why she'd reacted the way she did.

At first, she told herself it was because she was claustrophobic, but that wasn't true. She'd never had a problem with small spaces.

Then she tried to convince herself she'd thought he was going to fall on her and she'd just reacted to that. She even practiced bringing it up to him in a half-laughing way, saying something like, "Oh, don't trip onto me again!"

That, too, was a lie, and would probably only make things more awkward.

It took her two days to admit it to herself. The terrible, ugly, silly truth was Sheila hadn't kissed anyone since the divorce. It had been longer than that, even, since the passion had long gone out of their marriage before Brian had uttered those fateful words.

Six years, was it? Maybe seven years since a man had seen her as anything resembling an object of desire. Seven years since she'd felt the warmth of affection?

It was embarrassing. No wonder it had taken her so long to admit it to herself. Russell probably had women throwing themselves at him all the time.

A woman in every port – or airport. Whatever the modern equivalent was. Beautiful models in bikinis with glowing, tanned skin and impossibly long legs laid out on white sand beaches.

Nothing like homely Sheila, who spent her time running to the grocery store, scrubbing burnt-on sauce off pans, and dragging the garbage out to the curb. Her life wasn't the stuff of romance movies or picture-perfect Instagram pages.

"There's no way her life can really be that happy all the time..." she would mutter to herself as she scrolled by another blissful smiling woman before uploading another picture of lemon raspberry cookies to her own page.

Despite promising herself she wouldn't, Sheila went online and searched for information about Russell. There were many pictures of him with his stunning ex-wife, which she'd expected, but what she was really looking for was his own social media account, preferably on Instagram where he followed and flirted with dozens of models and actresses and proved her suspicions right.

Oddly, no such account existed. It seemed like he had no online presence at all, let alone one that proved him to be a lecherous creep.

Sheila slammed her laptop shut. She was projecting onto him. She had no idea what went on in his head, and she wasn't going to flatter herself into thinking he actually liked her.

The facts were obvious. He was a famous, handsome actor. He had tried to kiss her. It had happened, and she had reacted poorly.

The rest was less obvious. She didn't know if he'd only tried to kiss her because there were no other single women on the island. She didn't know if he was a playboy. She didn't know why her heart fluttered in her chest when he looked at her, or how to get herself to stop thinking about what it would be like to kiss his neck.

These were the things that would continue to keep her up at night.

. . .

There was only a week left before the big reopening for the tea shop and the cottage was overflowing with excitement. Patty was busy making three new recipes a day for the menu. Eliza had enlisted the help of her sisters to get an online presence for the tea shop by posting pictures, making adorable videos of Patty explaining the teas and the offerings, and promoting their first grand event: an open mic night.

Before Sheila could shoot the idea down, Eliza listed her as the headliner. **See Sheila Wilde in her first performance in seven years!**

"Eliza," Sheila hissed when she saw the pile of fliers on the kitchen table, "No one knows who I am, and I'm not going to headline the –"

"People remember you! When I posed this online, we got almost a thousand likes."

Sheila raised an eyebrow. "What? Why!"

"Because you're unforgettable," Eliza said with a wave of her hand. "Anyway, it makes us look cool to have a headliner."

As much as Sheila loved Eliza's revived spirit, she did not appreciate being a target of it. "Okay. As long as I don't have to sing."

Her smile fell away. "Mom. You have to sing."

"Eliza..." Sheila rubbed her face with her hands. "I'll host, but..."

"Please? Just one song. For me, Mom?"

Who was she to say no? Sheila was a sucker. She knew she was a sucker, and she'd never not be a sucker for her kids. "All right, one song. But only because I love you."

Eliza shrieked and threw her arms up for a hug. "I love you too, Mom!"

Before she agreed to anything else, Sheila disappeared upstairs to her bedroom and shut the door. What she really needed to do was finish Russell's taxes and budget.

She'd avoided it in an attempt to avoid thinking about him, but the least she could do was finish what she'd promised.

She sat down at her desk and opened the folder he'd given her. She filtered through the papers and added whatever she found to her slew of spreadsheets – income, payments, obligations.

There was a pile of papers clipped together with a Post-it note simply titled "Divorce." She poured over this, surprised to see he had declined alimony from his fabulously wealthy ex-wife. He'd also given up their Los Angeles home and agreed to sell their Minneapolis home.

In return, she'd left him a few assets. An old Jeep. A retirement account they'd both paid into. A company constantly referred to as only MMFL.

Sheila didn't remember him mentioning any companies. Was it a movie studio they'd started? The flower shop she'd always wanted? It seemed to still be in his possession, and it was draining money from him. There were large payments made for repairs, payments for taxes...

Flipping through the papers, she couldn't find the most basic information about it. She was going to make a note to ask him when she stumbled on a paper at the bottom of the bag. It must have fallen out of the divorce pile, this part of the agreement for Russell to take over partial ownership of MMFL.

Short for Marine Magic Funland.

Sheila held the paper in her hand as her blood ran cold.

Twenty-six

It was surprisingly easy to run from his problems. Russell managed to stay away for over a week, meeting up with friends and buying an endless number of things for the new house.

He couldn't believe how much stuff he didn't know he needed, like a smokeless fire pit and telescoping roasting forks. Carbon fishing rods. Kayaks and paddle boards to keep at the beach. An inflatable water climbing wall for the warmer months. A space-saving bed that folded up and out of the way.

He'd have to ask Mia if she was okay with the design aspect on that one, but really, all the purchases were for his kids. They were things to convince them to visit, to maybe make them so comfortable they wanted to stay a while.

Eventually, though, he had to get back to reality. His truck was packed full and, more importantly, it was opening night for the tea shop. He couldn't miss it, even if the idea of facing Sheila filled him with shame.

She had been the bigger person and reached out first; she'd texted to let him know she'd finished his expenses and budget.

"You weren't kidding," she'd written. "You're terrible with money, and at least now I know for a fact you can't afford to buy Patty's property."

He'd laughed out loud when he'd read it. Not just because it was true, but because she didn't seem to be holding a grudge. If she gave him another chance, he promised himself not to ruin their friendship, no matter how tempting it was. She was one of the few friends he'd made since the divorce, one of the few people he felt he could really trust, and that was worth everything.

He would learn to tame the feeling in his heart somehow. They probably sold something for it; he just hadn't found it yet.

As soon as he got home, he showered, put on his best flannel shirt, and walked over to the tea shop.

He heard the commotion before he saw it – voices, laughter, and music. It was chilly but the rain had held out, and as he got over the hill, he could see the patio filled with life.

There were older people, younger people, families with little ones, the kids running through the grass and onto the beach, kicking freezing water at each other. There were high schoolers in small, self-conscious groups, the loudest of them all.

The tea shop stood tall and sturdy, the new eggshell paint magnificent against the low-hanging evening sun. They were still a half hour from sunset, but the crisscrossing lights above the patio were ready and glowing, adding a whimsical feel to the already charming scene.

Russell skirted through the crowd, pulling his baseball cap low over his eyes to avoid detection. He didn't want to make this about him. He was here for Patty and Eliza.

And Sheila, of course.

He walked around to the front of the building and a new sign caught his eye: **A Spot of Tea.**

They'd taken his suggestion after all. He smiled and pulled the door open, stepping into the warm air filled with chatter and clanking of cups against saucers.

It looked like every table was full. People were standing in the lobby, sipping tea.

Eliza was at the register when she caught sight of him. "Hey!" She yelled. "Thanks for coming."

"Of course," he said.

She handed off a receipt, then picked up a tray piled with plates and cups. "It is crazy here tonight."

"Can I help you with that?" Russell asked, stepping forward.

Eliza didn't hesitate. "Sure!" She handed him the tray. "Patty's in the kitchen. You can just drop it off."

"No problem." Balancing the tray was the easy part; weaving through people's groups was harder than expected. He managed to get to the kitchen without falling over or dropping anything, and opened the swinging door to find Patty.

Her face lit up with a smile when she saw him. "Thank goodness you're here!" she said. "These people are insatiable! They've eaten every cookie I made, even the backups, and all but ten of the scones!"

"Sounds like it's going well, then," Russell said as he set the tray down on the counter. "Can I wash these or should I...?"

"No, no. You're not here to wash dishes." She grabbed him by the arm and pulled him toward the door. "I need to thank you properly for the work you had done on the cottage and the shop."

He tried to wriggle out of her grasp but she was surprisingly strong. "There's no need, I just wanted to –"

Patty cut him off, flinging the door open and putting her fingers in her mouth, letting out a resounding whistle.

The shop quieted.

"Hey everyone," she yelled, "Russell Westwood is here! He is a movie star, a wonderful neighbor, and he's available for pictures!"

Russell dropped his head down, grinning. "Well played," he said quietly.

"Thank you." She patted him on the arm. "We're even now."

She disappeared into the kitchen and Russell turned to find a small line forming ahead of him.

He cleared his throat. "Hi, everyone. Thanks for coming."

After half an hour, the line to take pictures with him had fizzled and Russell took the chance to slip outside. The sun had begun its descent and the clouds over the water were putting on quite a show, lined in orange and yellow with a hint of pink just starting at the horizon.

There were heaters outside with warm, enticing flames, but Russell took a seat on an empty bench on the outskirts. No one noticed him except for Derby, who was making the rounds and getting petted by anyone who would have him. He had a big red bow attached to his collar, and an older man held his leash.

Derby spotted Russell and dragged the old man over.

"Hey, buddy," he said, scratching his rump.

Derby rolled and put his paws up in the air. The old man laughed. "This guy is in heaven." He stuck out his hand. "I'm Reggie, Patty's friend."

"Nice to finally meet you. I'm Russell."

The old man's smile never broke. "I know. Sheila's friend."

A group of small children started pleading for Derby to come to them and he obliged, tugging at Reggie's arm.

He bowed his head slightly as he turned to leave. "Have a good evening."

There was still no sign of Sheila, but he knew he was in the right place. At the edge of the patio stood a small setup – two speakers, a microphone, and an electric keyboard. A small sign read, *Welcome to A Spot of Tea's open mic night!*

After ten minutes, he spotted her. She swooped in, wearing a black leather jacket, and glided to the microphone, her hair blowing in the breeze.

She tapped on it to get the crowd to quiet. "Hi, everyone. Thank you so much for coming out tonight. I'm Sheila Wilde."

There were a few yells and *woo*s from the audience.

Sheila nodded and pointed out at the crowd. "Thank you to my fans. You two mean the world to me."

Now everyone laughed.

She smiled that hesitant smile, the one that always drew him in. "It really does mean a lot to us that you're here tonight. I don't know all of you, but I'm guessing most of you know Patty, who owns the tea shop. You might know there have been more than a few hard times around here." She paused and a smile spread across her face. "All I can say is we're *so* happy to bring this place back to life with the help of all you good people."

Russell started to clap, and everyone followed suit.

Sheila took a seat at the keyboard and adjusted the microphone. "I've been bullied into kicking off the open mic tonight because, as you may know, Patty is my mother-in-law, and moving in with her has been a dream come true. I've finally realized my role as a failed artist."

Laughter erupted again, bouncing through the crowd as patrons from inside filtered out and filled in the gaps on the patio.

Sheila grinned, and Russell grinned back at her. She hadn't seen him yet—at least he didn't think she had—but he could see her, her eyes twinkling under the hanging lights, the ocean at her back, the sunset providing the most brilliant backdrop.

"I promised my daughter I would sing one song, so here we go."

She turned to the piano and struck the first note, soft and sweet.

Oh daughter, oh daughter of mine
When did you learn to speak when spoken to?

Oh daughter, my darling, so fine
When you're silent, there's always a why

A few months ago, on his first kayak trip around the island, Russell had gotten pulled in by a deep current. He didn't realize what was happening until he looked up and saw how far he was from shore.

Here it was, happening again. He sat staring at her profile, softly illuminated by the twinkling lights, casting a gentle shadow on her delicate features. Her eyes, so soft yet focused on the music, sparkled and danced over every note.

The crowd had fallen silent, even the shrieking children, everyone suspended in a moment of awe as her beautiful melody filled the night air.

She sang on, each note rising from the depths of her heart, the starlit canopy opening above them as the sun disappeared behind the horizon.

He couldn't help but be captivated by her. He couldn't stop himself from being carried away, nor did he want to. Sheila wasn't a current. Sheila was the entire sea.

Twenty-seven

Applause poured from the crowd and Sheila lifted her fingers from the keys. She'd promised Eliza one song and she was sticking to it, but she was tempted to keep going.

There was something magical about performing. Just before she'd begun, a silence had hung between her and the audience, like an agreement to listen, to understand. It was something she had missed so badly, the feeling of being heard.

The adrenaline flowed through her veins now and she stood up, grinning like a fool.

It was time to go. "Thank you, everyone!" Sheila said into the microphone. "Up next, I'd like to welcome my good friend Reggie, who has a poem to share with us."

Reggie handed off Derby's leash and approached the makeshift stage. "That was beautiful," he said into her ear.

"Thank you," she whispered as she handed him the microphone.

"Hello, everyone," he said in his slow and steady voice. "I'm going to be reading a poem by Wendy Cope. It's called 'The Orange.'"

Sheila floated through the audience as people patted her on her back, pulling her into whisper compliments.

It was too much. She caught sight of Eliza and Patty by the door and rushed to them.

"That was *amazing*, Mom," Eliza said, hugging her.

"Thanks, sweetie. It was for you, you know."

Her daughter smiled. "I know."

Patty had her eyes on Reggie, a bemused look on her face. As soon as he finished reading his poem, she blew him a kiss, then rushed them inside the tea shop. "Quick! Before someone asks me for a scone."

Inside, there were only a few people remaining at the tables and the lobby was entirely deserted.

"Thank goodness the entertainment started," Patty said. "We've almost run out of all our baked treats. I did not expect this many people."

"To be honest, I didn't either," Eliza said, "and I'm the one who planned the whole thing."

Sheila had to hold back from telling Eliza she might've found her calling. It was better she arrive at that conclusion herself. "You did wonderfully. I'm so proud of you."

Eliza's eyes shot down, but she smiled. "Thanks, Mom."

"I'm proud of both of you!" Patty said. "I swear, this place was weeks away from being condemned until you stubborn goats decided to turn it around."

"I get my stubbornness from you," Eliza said.

"Baa!" Sheila added, and they burst into laughter.

Patty shushed her and said, "Good. A woman needs her stubbornness. It keeps the world from rolling her over."

"I didn't know there was a goat in here," said a voice from behind.

Sheila sucked in a breath.

Russell.

She turned, and as much as she thought she was prepared for this moment, seeing him still took her breath away.

He was undeniably the best-looking person she'd ever seen close up, but it was more than that. There was something else, something she had not realized until this moment, until she felt a smolder in her chest.

"Well, if it isn't our celebrity relief!" Patty put a hand on his chest. "Oh, that's firm. You're big on the exercise, aren't you?"

He laughed and patted her hand. "I hope my being here was more helpful than distracting."

"Of course it was," she said. "I hope you're not too upset at me for throwing you to the wolves."

Russell would love nothing more than to be thrown to wolves. Sheila met his eyes and they smiled.

Eliza raised an eyebrow. "What'd you do, Granny?"

"Nothing!" she said in a high-pitched voice. "I just gave the people what they wanted."

"She blew my cover," Russell said, then let out a laugh. "I was happy to help."

"Good." Patty said, then grabbed Eliza by the arm. "I need you to come with me."

"Why?" Eliza tried to rip her arm away, but Patty was not stopping. "Can we –"

"Come along now!" She said peppily, leading Eliza away.

Normally, Sheila would've felt embarrassed at this obvious ploy, but she was too busy grappling with other things, like the realization that Russell held her heart in his hands, and that she'd sent him a threatening email about a whale she hadn't known he partially owned.

The fact that he knew neither of these things made her feel absolutely panicked.

"Hey," he said, his beautiful blue eyes locked on her. "That performance was incredible. *You're* incredible."

Her usual instinct was to dismiss any compliments, but she stopped herself and said, "Thank you. It was honestly the best I've felt in ages."

"You belong on the stage," he said before taking a step closer to her, lowering his voice. "Can we talk? In private?"

Oh no. *He knew.* He knew she was the one who sent the email.

Her heart pounded against her ribs. This wasn't how she wanted to tell him, but it was happening. She had to go with it. "Sure. In the kitchen?"

He nodded and she led the way through the door and into the cozy little space. Gold-rimmed teacups were stacked in the sink, and plates with crumbs and jam were piled on the counters.

No, she couldn't do it. She didn't have the words. She had to change the subject. "How was your trip off island?"

"It was good. Spent more money." He laughed. "You probably could have guessed."

"Yes. That tracks." She smiled. "I finished making a budget for you."

He winced. "Ah, a budget. How bad of shape am I in?"

This was far easier to deliver. "Pretty bad. You need to do another movie, or a product endorsement, or something."

He sighed. "Yeah, sure. We can figure it out."

We. Did he trust her to make those decisions for him?

"There's something else I wanted to say to you. Needed to say to you."

Sheila couldn't break her eyes away from him. "Okay."

"It's about the day before I left. At my house. I wanted to apologize..."

Her heart leapt. So she hadn't imagined it. He had been trying to kiss her.

"It's fine," she said, putting up a hand. "Honestly. Like, not a big deal. Happens all the time."

Happens all the time? As though clients were falling over themselves to try to kiss her?

A smile faltered on his lips. "Well, you know, it's..." He shook his head. "I'm sorry. I'm bad at this."

She laughed. "It's okay. I get it."

"I value you. As a friend. I like having you as a neighbor, too. And..."

He trailed off again.

No wonder he was an actor. He really did need someone to write his lines for him.

She interrupted his struggle. "As a bookkeeper?"

Russell laughed. "Yes. That too."

"I was happy to help you with that. You weren't as messy as many clients I've had in the past."

"Oh?" He nodded. "That's good to know."

Maybe this was how she could tell him? He clearly wasn't too sensitive about his expenses. He probably didn't care about the park – it was a product of the divorce. What were the chances he even knew Lottie existed?

Yes, this was how she could tell him the truth. "You've got some interesting assets."

He crossed his arms over his chest. "I didn't think of you as the judgmental type."

Sheila laughed. "I'm not! But that amusement park? With that whale? I mean, honestly, you're better off getting out of that."

He groaned. "Yeah. It's been a sore spot. I've spent a lot on it."

"I saw." She paused. "Maybe it's best to shut it down. All that maintenance...and let that whale go, too."

He was quiet for a moment. "The whale?"

"She's probably your worst asset. I don't judge the others, but that one..." She made a face.

"That bad, huh?" he said, his voice soft.

"Not bad, no," she said. "It's just, you know, she..." Sheila sighed. "She's – I wanted to talk to you about her."

"About Lottie."

Oh. So he did know her name. "Yes. You know, orcas are a lot like wolves. They live in families, and removing one from a family is detrimental. Think of what would've happened in

Yellowstone if Wolf 8 had been captured and forced to perform circus tricks."

He was silent.

She couldn't stop talking. "Funnily enough, there's actually a group ready to retire her. They want to build a sea pen and she could rejoin her family right here near the islands –"

Russell interrupted her. "How do you know that?" A line had formed across his forehead. His eyes were narrowed, and his mouth was a thin line.

It felt like a brick sank in her chest. "I saw it online."

"No, you didn't." He took a step back. "What is this, Sheila?"

"It's..." Her voice faltered. "Financial advice."

He stared at her. "Was this all part of your plan? Befriending me, making you think you cared about me and the wolves all to –"

"I didn't plan anything," she said firmly, because that was entirely the truth.

Russell ran a hand through his hair. "Who sent that email, Sheila?"

Oh no. This wasn't how she wanted it to go at all. "You have to believe me, Russell. I had no idea you owned Lottie."

He put his hands up and backed away. "I don't know what to believe. It feels a lot like I'm the mark here."

She shook her head. "No. I'm not that much of a mastermind. Believe me."

Russell shook his head. "This is my fault, really. I should know better."

"Please." She sucked in a breath. "It's not what you think."

"You know what's interesting? Holly said that same thing to me once." Her throat was dry and when she tried to respond, she only coughed. "Right before she left me for Hank. It's funny how it's not what I think, except it always is."

He turned and disappeared through the door.

Sheila stood, staring. It was as though she'd dropped whatever they had and it had shattered into a million pieces around her feet.

Her vision blurred. There was no way to put it back together again.

Twenty-eight

I t was a rule of nature that the highest of highs preceded the lowest of lows, the mountains and the valleys, the yin and the yang.

Eliza had felt something coming. Her life had started to change for the better: work excited her, every day flexing skills she didn't know she had, and she saw the rewards of her labor with her own eyes.

For the first time in her adult life, she was able to help someone – *really* help them – so it shouldn't have surprised her that everything would come crashing down.

What was surprising was how quickly it happened.

The cracks started to form less than twenty-four hours after re-opening at the tea shop. She'd stayed up late that night cleaning the shop and marveling at the reviews pouring in. People loved the food, the tea, and the sassy grandma serving it, and they loved the entertainment. It was, by all accounts, a raging success.

The next morning, she was awakened by a phone call from her grandma – her other grandma, her mom's mom.

"Is everything okay, Eliza?" she asked, putting extra emphasis on the word "okay."

Eliza sat up in bed, bleary-eyed, and pulled on her glasses. She couldn't remember the last time she'd even talked to Grandma. Was it three years ago, when she'd crashed Christmas Eve wearing a robe and insisting they hold a masquerade-themed Christmas? Or was it someone's birthday, maybe Emma's, when she'd rode in on the back of a motorcycle, hanging onto her new tattooed boyfriend and complaining about the lack of cupcakes?

"We're fine, Grandma. How are you?"

"I'm at the house and no one is here! I thought I'd stop by for your mom's birthday."

She was several weeks too late, but there was no need to point that out. "We're staying up with Granny on San Juan Island. Thanks for thinking of us, though!"

There were voices downstairs, and the smell of something delicious from the oven. She'd overslept. Was that cinnamon?

Grandma sighed. "I tried calling your mom this morning, but she didn't answer. I'm very worried."

"She's just downstairs. There's nothing to worry about."

"I have bad news, Eliza!" Grandma said. "You have to tell her to call me back."

She pulled on the fluffy pink robe Granny had gotten for her a week after she'd moved in. "Okay, I will."

"I mean right away! It's time sensitive."

"Okay."

"Eliza," Grandma said sternly, "it's about the house. I don't want your mom to be upset, but I opened some of the mail sitting out here."

Of course she had. "Sure thing, Grandma. I'll go down and tell her. She's been busy, so it might take her a few days to get back to you."

"No, you're not listening to me!" Grandma dropped her voice to a whisper. "There's a notice of default for the house! She needs to call the bank right away. Thank goodness I was here to find it."

Eliza wasn't sure exactly what it meant, but she knew it had to be a mistake. Her mom had never defaulted on anything. "I'm sure it's nothing, but thank you. I'll let Mom know."

"Thanks. Is there a spare key hidden somewhere? I need a place to rest."

Eliza promised to check with her mom and managed to end the call before running down the stairs and finding her mom and Granny enjoying morning tea.

"The raspberry cheese danishes aren't quite ready, sweetie," Granny said when she saw her. "Should I start some coffee for you?"

"Thanks, Granny, but I'll have tea." She took a teacup from the cupboard and sat down. "Mom, I just got a call from Grandma."

Her mom made a face. "Oh. I haven't heard from her in ages. I tried calling her a few weeks ago, but her phone number was disconnected."

Nothing unusual for Grandma. She didn't like to be tied down, preferring to swoop in like an exotic bird and surprise them all. When she was younger, Eliza thought she was great.

As she got older, though, she realized what life must've been like for her mom, and it didn't seem so fun.

"She thinks there's some mistake with the house."

"Oh?" Sheila set her tea down. "What kind of mistake?"

"Something with the bank. She was opening our mail and found a notice of default for the house. And she wants to know where you've hidden the spare key."

"Hm. I'll have to call her."

"Oh!" Granny stood from her chair. "That reminds me, I got another letter from the insurance company."

Her mom tilted her head to the side. "I thought I sorted that all out."

"I thought so, too. I'll go get it."

For the first time since she came downstairs, Eliza really looked at her mom. She had bags under her eyes and her expression was flat. "Is everything okay, Mom?"

She smiled. "Of course. Just a little tired from yesterday."

Granny returned with an envelope in her hand. "This is it! They keep harassing me, Sheila. I told you they were!"

Her mom popped the envelope open and pulled out the stack of papers inside, carefully unfolding them. "This isn't from the insurance company."

Granny frowned, hands on her hips. "It isn't? I thought it was."

Sheila's eyes scanned the first page, then she quickly folded it up and tucked it back in the envelope. "It's fine. I'll look into it."

"Well, what do they want?" Granny asked. "They said they were going to liquidate."

"It's just some confusion. Nothing to worry about."

She picked up her teacup with both hands and turned to Eliza. "I'll give your grandma a call. I'm guessing she has nowhere to stay."

"Sounds good. I'll text you the number she called me from."

She left, and Eliza felt a pressure settle into her chest. She didn't know what it was, but something was off. Her mom was hiding something.

It was time to call in her sisters and see what they knew.

Twenty-nine

He thought he must be getting sick, or having a heart attack, or both. Every time Russell closed his eyes, he saw Sheila's face and his chest would constrict, like a vise around his heart. His breath was heavy, a chill ran to his core, and sweat pooled on his brow.

He couldn't stand staying at his house. By noon the next morning, Russell was halfway to Arizona. One of his fellow wolf enthusiasts had invited him to visit ages ago, but he'd never had the time to make the trip.

Then, two days ago, the guy left a breathless voicemail with some news. "One of the female wolves traveled north, *far* north. Above I-40!" he'd said. "We think she's looking for a mate. She could make it to Colorado."

Looking for love. Russell thought she'd be better off staying at home.

Nevertheless, he needed to get away from the island, and he wanted to learn more about the Mexican gray wolf population. They were stunning little creatures, the smallest wolves in North America, and had been totally wiped out by the 1970's. It wasn't until 1998 that conservationists had reintroduced eleven of them into the wilds of Arizona.

Now, a quarter century later, there were nearly three hundred wolves living, hunting, and playing in Arizona and New Mexico. They were thriving and doing so in a new world that had seemed impossibly hostile to them a short time ago.

It was inspiring and even if his mood was sour, he could be thrilled for the little wolf venturing out of her comfort zone.

When he got to Phoenix, Russell rented a car and made a call to the realtor who'd sold him his place on San Juan Island.

"I think I'm ready to put the house back on the market," he told her.

"Oh no!" She groaned. "You don't like it? Are you sure you've given it enough of a chance?"

"I'm sure. Let's list it."

Driving always helped clear his head, but this time, it wasn't working. His thoughts were thick with regret.

Why did he think he could trust anyone, especially someone who had showed up in his life so randomly, pretending to be a friend? Who was he to think he could live like a normal person? That he could move to a new place and build a new life?

It was impossible. The stain of his career would never leave him. People looked at him and saw one thing: an opportunity.

Read my script. Loan me a million. Free my whale.

At least Sheila had been original. He could give her that. He wouldn't have expected someone to fake a friendship with him to get to a *whale*.

The things people wanted from him were endless, and he couldn't anticipate what would come next. There was no chance at real friendship for him. There was no chance of falling in love. He was ashamed he'd even allowed his mind to go there. Not that he'd had much of a choice, but still.

Until he could accept that he was never going to be part of a community again, he'd be the perfect target. It was best if he sold everything and moved to a cabin in the woods. The kids could still visit, and at least he'd get to see the wolves once in a while.

His phone rang, and for a moment, his traitorous heart hoped it might be Sheila. "Hello?"

"Hey, Russ," the familiar voice said. "It's Holly."

He stopped himself from saying, *Just what I needed. A call from you.* There was no need to spread his misery. Instead, he went with, "Hey, Holly."

"I don't have a lot of time to talk, so I'll just get to it." Her voice was tentative, polite. "I don't think I'm going to be able to do Thanksgiving, and I feel awful."

Ah. As he'd expected. "Where are you shooting that movie again?"

"We're in Vancouver. It's really nice, but yeah. We're running behind and the studio wants us to do some reshoots. It's a mess."

Life could still be worse. He could still be answering to studio executives. Russell didn't miss that in the least. "That's not too far from my place on San Juan Island."

"Oh yeah? You ended up moving there after all? I know Mia mentioned it."

"I did."

He tried to keep the edge out of his voice. It wasn't her fault she'd moved on and didn't keep track of what he was doing with his life. It wasn't her fault he was discarded goods no one wanted. She was just the first person to identify it.

He cleared his throat. "Listen, I don't know if this would be too weird, but I could host. You could book a plane. It can't be more than an hour or two, fly back after dinner."

"Are you serious, Russ? That would be...I mean, just amazing." She paused. "There's just one thing."

He knew what it was, but he had to play nice. "What's that?"

"Toby – uh, the guy I'm seeing. We were supposed to spend Thanksgiving together. I don't know if you know him. Toby McFlaren." She laughed. "I think you two would get along."

As if he didn't know who Toby McFlaren was. He'd won two Golden Globes for his depiction of a prisoner of war in *Battleship Echoes,* and he'd been voted sexiest man alive last year.

"The big guy? I've seen him." He paused. "Bring him along. I can put him to work chopping some wood. Maybe carrying plywood around."

Holly laughed, a real one this time. "Do you mean it, Russ? Oh, this would just – I've been so torn up about this."

It was what was best for Lucas and Mia. It was only a matter of time before both of them married and took off on their own. How many more Thanksgiving dinners would they have as a family?

He wasn't trying to win Holly back; he was past that.

Sure, if he could wake up and find out it had all been a bad dream, he would take it in a heartbeat. But it was too late to win her back. Too much had changed. He had changed.

People liked to ask if he was "over" the divorce. A divorce wasn't something to get across, like a bridge. It was something completely transformative, like a bomb going off.

He was still here, his heart beating in his chest, getting ideas of its own.

He could forgive Holly, even envy her, with her full life, with her joy. She had no fear of loving again.

Russell was different. Maybe he was overreacting to Sheila trying to get something out of him. He wasn't sure. He couldn't think about it. It was too painful to picture her face, her smile, her laugh...

It was too painful to know he'd been living with a false hope – that he could trust again, even live again.

The best he could do was be a gracious ex-husband. "The more the merrier," he said.

Thirty

As soon as she could do so without attracting suspicion, Sheila made an excuse to retreat upstairs to the privacy of her bedroom.

First, she called her mom back and told her where to find the spare key to the house.

"Please don't worry about me," her mom, the stoic, said. "I will make myself at home and make do."

Sheila sighed. "Sounds good, Mom."

Of course her mom would show up at a moment like this. She could be a lot of fun when she was around, but she wasn't helpful in a crisis. She was more like the harbinger of a crisis.

Sheila ended the call, then tried to focus. She couldn't bear to think past this moment or she'd end up sick to her stomach like the night before.

She gripped Patty's letter in her hand so tightly that it hurt. If only she could crush the thing, strike it from existence – but the best she could do was call the number listed.

The flat voice on the line confirmed what she'd feared. Patty hadn't been getting threatening letters from the insurance company; she'd been getting threatening letters from the bank. Ray had taken out a business loan before his death, and Patty hadn't made a payment in years.

"So you're saying," Sheila said, her voice shaking, "unless we can come up with a hundred thousand dollars by next month, you are going to liquidate the business?"

"That is what you agreed to when you signed for the loan," the woman responded. "Is there anything else I can help you with today?"

"No. That was all."

Sheila ended the call and stared down at the floor.

There had to be a way out of this. After all they'd done, they couldn't lose the tea shop. Patty couldn't lose her home and her life. Eliza couldn't lose what she'd worked so hard to build. There had to be something she could do.

But it wasn't Sheila's only problem. A notice of default for the house meant her time had run out. The house would soon be foreclosed. It could be a matter of weeks or months, but she was going to lose that too.

She just needed a little time! The tea shop was going to be profitable. That much was obvious. Maybe she could work out a payment plan with the bank? Maybe she could take out another loan? Her sisters would loan her the money, but both of them were broke, too. It was like a family curse. Would they ever escape it?

There was one option she had been avoiding. One she hadn't even wanted to consider, one she thought she never would stoop low enough to do.

But there was no place for her pride. Sheila picked up her phone and dialed.

No answer.

She stood, pacing across the room before sitting back down on the bed. She called again.

"Sheila?" he asked. "Is this a crank call?"

At least he was in a good mood. "Hi, Brian. No, I need to talk to you."

"Whew boy. This sounds serious." He laughed. "Trouble in paradise?"

She let out a slow breath. "Things are going pretty well here, actually. Really well. We reopened the tea shop last night. Had a great turnout."

"Good for you."

"Eliza did an amazing job with the website and planning the event. Your mom is really happy, Brian."

"That's good, I guess. Is there a point to this call?"

Instead, she gritted her teeth and said, "There's a problem."

"What's that?"

"Ray took out a loan before he died. I don't think your mom realized she signed it, but now they want to liquidate the tea shop and sell everything off. Maybe even the property. I'm not sure yet."

He let out a gruff laugh. "Of course they do. That's how business loans work when you don't pay them. I thought you were supposed to know these things?"

"We just need some time, Brian. I need a little help making the payments, but then the shop is going to take off and –"

"You're unbelievable, you know that? You got my mom's hopes up and then you come begging me for money?"

"I'm not begging."

"I thought you were supposed to be good with money? Why don't you pay it?"

"Because I've been putting four daughters through college," she snapped. "Without any help from you."

"We don't believe in babying our kids."

We. He meant his new wife Kylie, who liked to tell everyone her parents hadn't helped her pay for school and how much stronger it had made her.

Brian embraced her mythology fully, while still living in a house they'd bought for her.

"It's not babying. It's supporting."

He continued. "Is that what this is about? You're bitter because the child support ran dry?"

Sheila's chest heaved with each breath and she had to force herself to respond calmly. "No. This is about your mother needing a little help."

"You know what? I'm happy to help her. Of course I will."

Her voice caught in her throat. "You will?"

"Yeah. I'll help her sell that place at a profit and move somewhere more appropriate for her age."

Oh, she could *scream*.

"I've got to go. Have a nice day, Sheila," he said.

The line went dead, and she was left there feeling like a boat untied from its dock.

Thirty-one

After the grand opening, Patty was busy – wonderfully, steadily busy – and she wouldn't have it any other way.

It was a lot, surely, but the steady flow of customers was manageable with Eliza's help. Patty started her day at five, just as she liked, baking old favorites and crafting new creations. They opened the tea shop at eight and Reggie was the first in the door. Their regulars followed soon after for a cup of tea, a biscuit, and a chat.

It filled her heart with joy to hear the little bells ringing on the tables. More bells meant more tea, which meant more talking about tea, and whale sightings, and the ever-changing weather.

Against all odds, the tea shop was alive again. It was more than a coat of paint and an overdue cleaning – it was filled with *love,* and no matter how tired she felt, the warmth of this place kept her going.

Nothing could be better. Or at least, so she thought. Two weeks after the grand opening, Patty was busy, rushing around, her heart so full that she could hardly understand the sound she heard coming from inside the cottage.

She normally didn't return to the cottage mid-morning, but she'd spilled a vat of cream on herself and needed to change.

It was quiet, but sharp and erratic, carrying down the hallway.

It sounded like crying.

But who could be crying when life was so wonderful?

She paused in the hallway and listened, touching a hand to her hearing aid. Perhaps it was malfunctioning, or perhaps the neighbor's cat had gotten into the house again.

Patty leaned into Sheila's closed door and heard the distinct sound of a nose blowing almost comically loud.

"Is there a clown with a cold in there?" Patty called out.

Silence, and then, "Hi, sorry, I'll be down in a minute."

Patty frowned. Sheila really had been crying. She wasn't a crier – not since the divorce. Back then, Patty had heard her cry almost every day, though she never let on that she knew.

Of course, Patty always knew.

"I'm coming in!" she announced.

"No!" Sheila said. "I'm not decent."

"Not decent," Patty grumbled, opening the door. "I watched you bring four lives into this world. I don't think you're going to shock me now."

But what she saw when she opened the door did shock her. There was a pile of tissues spilling from the bed onto the floor. Sheila sat on the bed with papers scattered around her. Her shoulders were slumped downward, her eyes red and small.

Mascara streaked down her face in splattered black stripes, as though she'd put on makeup only to immediately cry it off.

"My darling! Whatever is the matter?" Patty said, rushing to her side.

Sheila was quiet for a moment. "Oh, you know. Everything."

Patty wrapped an arm around her. "It can't be that bad."

"I've failed you, Patty. I've failed you, and the girls, and Lottie. I've ruined everything." She kept her eyes down, focused on the tissue she was decimating with her fingers.

"Well. It sounds like we're going to need some tea. I'll boil the kettle."

. . .

It took Patty nearly half an hour to convince Sheila to tell her what had happened.

When she was done, Sheila sat staring at the teacup in her hands. "I thought we'd be able to keep the house and the tea shop, Patty. I was sure we'd find a way."

"You did find a way." Patty chuckled. "I'm just a dope who didn't know she'd signed a loan."

"You're not a dope."

Patty waved a hand. "We can find a way out. I'll call the bank."

"I already tried that. They won't work with us unless we have the money. They said it's too late."

"Don't worry about me." She sighed. "I knew this day was coming. But wow, did you give me a beautiful send off." Patty smiled, but Sheila didn't return it.

"I've lost your house. I've lost my house. Russell thinks I'm some eco-terrorist mastermind, and Lottie will never get home." She was quiet for a moment before adding. "Brian was right. I'm nothing without him."

Patty pursed her lips. "Now you hold on right there. Brian was *not* right. I cannot believe he said that!"

"I'm sorry." Sheila shook her head and drew herself up. "I shouldn't have told you."

"Yes, you should have. I'm going to give him a piece of my mind, but first, we're going to get some help. We'll figure this out."

"Please, Patty," Sheila grabbed her hand. "Don't tell anyone. I can't bear it. I'm going to tell the girls soon, but – please. Promise me you won't tell anyone."

Patty stared at her, her lips pursed. "Fine." She crossed her fingers in her apron pocket. "I promise."

Thirty-two

There was something uncanny about the knocking on Russell's door.

It wasn't that it was unusually loud or unusually hard – in fact, it was so soft he had mistaken it for a woodpecker at first.

What disturbed him was the persistence. The knocker started knocking and kept going, and though he called out, "Coming," the knocking didn't stop. It went on and on the entire time it took him to finish rinsing the soap off the pan in the sink, dry his hands, and rush to unbolt the lock.

All the while, he knew it wasn't Sheila. She hadn't tried to contact him again, and he'd nearly convinced himself it was better that way.

Nearly. As much as he told himself it was better she stayed away, and her being absent proved how guilty she was, that she'd never cared for him at all outside of trying to use him...he still wondered.

Could it have all been a misunderstanding? How much of a fool would he have to be to believe their meeting was a coincidence, and she hadn't known he owned Lottie, that she hadn't been plotting all along?

It was hard to believe people didn't know everything about him. It seemed like his personal details were plastered on the internet for everyone to see.

Yet despite all of that, despite the gaping hole in his chest, late at night, when he knew he wouldn't be disturbed, he put her music on and listened with his eyes closed.

He finally opened the door and the knocker stood, her hand still suspended in midair.

"Patty?" He blinked at her. "Is everything okay?"

"No, it is not," she said curtly. "Can I come in?"

Before he could answer, she pushed by him and walked into the kitchen.

"You scared me," he said, closing the front door and joining her at the kitchen island. "I thought a tiny bird was trying to warn me my house was on fire."

"It's much worse than that," Patty said. She took a seat at one of the kitchen stools and glided a hand across the counter. "It's very beautiful what you've done with the place."

"Thank you, I –"

"But I'm not here for pleasantries," Patty added, cutting him off. "You are making a big mistake, buddy."

Buddy? He knew he shouldn't, but he cracked a smile. "Do you think? I didn't think the new rosebush was that bad, but if you hate it –"

"I'm talking about Sheila." Patty snapped, her eyes locked on his.

"I know." He sighed. He needed to stay firm. It didn't matter how much he missed Sheila, how he ached to hear her laugh again. In fact, it was only more important he stay away from her. He was weak when it came to her. "Listen, Patty, I appreciate what you're trying to do, but I think it's best if we all just let it go."

"Oh, *you* think it's best, do you?" She sucked in a breath and pointed a finger inches from his nose. "Let me tell you something, young man. I've been around a long time, and I don't care if you're a big Hollywood star. I know a lot more about this life than you do."

"Yes, but –"

"No buts! I'm not done yet."

Russell shut his mouth and resolved to keep it shut.

Patty went on. "Sheila told me what happened. Or at least, as much as she could tell me. I had to pry it out of her." She shook her head. "That is a woman who would not ask for help if her hair was on fire. And I know this because I'm a lot like her."

As well-intentioned as this was, they were not school children who needed their mother to intervene. There were things that couldn't be fixed sometimes.

He happened to be one of those things.

"We had a disagreement," Russell said gently. "It doesn't matter in the end. I'm selling the house after Thanksgiving."

She didn't take her eyes off him. She clasped her hands together and slightly tilted her head to the side. "That woman is in love with you."

If only. "I don't think I see it."

Her glare continued. "It doesn't matter how old you get. You men can't see anything." Patty shook her head and *tsk*ed. "Sheila will do anything for the ones she loves."

"Be that as it may, you might not be aware of all of her intentions," he said firmly. "I don't want to be rude, but –"

"You are being rude." Patty stood. "Don't you see? Sheila made a promise to that whale, years ago. It had nothing to do with you. Then, because life can be so twisted, she met *you*, of all people, and fell in love with you. You fell in love with her, too. Don't deny it. I saw how you looked at her when she was singing."

He stared at her, his mind tumbling over her words. Was he that obvious? That much of a rube?

The image of her singing under the twinkling lights filled his mind and his breath caught in his throat.

"She's in trouble, you know. Of course you don't know." Patty waved a hand. "You're not speaking to her, but you should be! She's going to lose her house, and she's terrified to tell the girls, and now we're going to lose the tea shop too."

The thought of her with her back to the sunset dashed from his mind as his stomach sunk. "The tea shop? Why?"

She clenched her jaw, grumbled, and released it. "It doesn't matter." Her voice softened. "The shop is just a thing, Russell. You have to understand. We can lose things; we can get things. Love is far more rare, and far more important."

The more she talked about love, the room spun. He heaved himself onto a kitchen stool.

It took him a moment to speak again. "I can't, Patty. I just can't."

She stared at him, the wrinkles around her eyes pulling together. "I know you've had your heart broken." She put a hand on his shoulder. "Do you think you're the only one?"

In that moment, he stopped trying to argue. She reminded him so much of his own mom, the yelling included. He'd never needed his mom's sage advice more than in the last five years, but she'd been gone nearly a decade.

"How do I know it's real? With Sheila. How can I be sure?"

"My dear boy!" A smile spread across Patty's face, a twinkle in her eye. "Don't you know? There is no love without risk, and there is no life without love."

Ah. Everything went back to that: stomach-churning, sleep-stealing, life-threatening risk.

There was no use in asking Patty anything more about it. She was convinced she knew what was best – convinced Sheila did, in fact, love him.

How could she know? It was impossible. He'd been obvious about how he felt – so obvious that even his elderly neighbor could see it.

As far as they knew, Sheila could be fooling them both. The thought made him want to run – get in the car right now and get off the island.

Russell stood from his seat. "Would you like some tea?"

Patty, apparently satisfied she'd ruined his morning, hugged him and said, "No, thank you," before walking out the door.

Russell stood there, mug in hand, feeling as hollowed out as the doorway, open to the expansive of blue sky above.

Thirty-three

A fter a week of talking – pleading – with the bank, Sheila had her final answer. There was no way to keep the tea shop unless they came up with a hundred thousand dollars to pay off the loan.

The truth of it hung like a weight on her neck. She walked stooped over, her eyes downcast and her spirit extinguished.

Sheila was so low that she could finally face calling the bank about the foreclosure notice on her home. It wasn't as dire – she had some options. Apparently, banks didn't like to foreclose on homes. Not for any benevolent reason, but because it cost them money.

If she came up with enough cash, she could hold them off, but it would mean going back to the mainland and getting a job as quickly as possible. It would mean giving up on this dream they'd all shared.

Why not pretend it was fine for a bit longer?

During the day, she could keep up the act, but at night, her mind wandered. She stared at the ceiling, her heart miles away in the tiny tank where Lottie slept, alone, her calls absorbed by the darkness.

That morning Brian called, but Sheila missed it entirely. She was engrossed with job postings, wondering how she'd explain her recent firing in an interview, when she saw he'd left a voicemail.

"How dare you go after my mother!" he spat. "You bankrupted her business and now you're losing our house, too? Great work, Sheila. Top notch. I guess I shouldn't have expected anything different from you. Know this: I'm not giving you a dime."

Blood rushed to her face and burned her cheeks. She gritted her teeth and deleted the voicemail.

Our house. How could he refer to it as his? As if she hadn't almost lost everything to buy him out of it.

She ran downstairs. "Patty, did you tell Brian about the tea shop?"

Patty pulled off her oven mitts, a pan of raspberry short-cake scones cooling on the oven. "Not exactly."

"Then how does he know? He thinks I bankrupted you."

"Oh." She nodded. "That might've been because of me. I asked if he would help you with the payments on the house. I didn't tell him about the tea shop, exactly, just that I've got some loans here I can't cover..." She shrugged. "It seems he jumped to some conclusions."

It didn't matter. His facts weren't right, but the result was the same: they were going to lose everything.

Sheila sat down at the table. "I'm so sorry, Patty. I failed you."

"Stop saying that! Who knows? Maybe Reggie will propose and I'll move in with him!" She cackled and took a seat, her face lit by a bright smile. "Don't worry about me. I'll be fine. I keep telling you that, and I mean it."

Her phone lit up again. Thankfully, it wasn't Brian – it was her eldest daughter Mackenzie on a video call.

Sheila took a deep breath before forcing a smile and answering. "Hey Mack!"

"Hey Mom! Where are you?"

She panned her phone over to the scones. "I'm at Granny's house. How are you?"

Mackenzie waved a hand. "I'm good. I wanted to come visit. Soon."

That weight on her chest pushed deeper. "Oh yeah? To Granny's?"

There was a knock at the back door. Patty put a hand on her shoulder. "You stay put. I'll get it."

Sheila watched the door open to two smiling faces: Shelby and Emma.

Her jaw dropped. "Girls! I didn't know you were coming!"

Eliza walked in behind them, a grin on her face. "Surprise! You weren't supposed to know, Mom. This is an intervention."

Sheila already had the girls in a hug and she had to pull away. "What?"

Patty spun around with a plate of blueberry cream cheese muffins in her hand. "I made intervention muffins!"

"I don't know why you would –"

Mackenzie, still on the screen, cut her off. "The jig is up, Mom. Eliza told us about the house, and Granny filled us in on the rest."

Patty locked eyes with her, beaming. "Guilty. Who wants tea?"

"Sit down, Mom," Eliza said gently. "We need to talk."

. . .

It took a full hour to tell them everything, going back to when Sheila met Lottie.

"I can't believe you got fired," Shelby said.

"I can't believe you broke into an amusement park," Emma said.

Mackenzie, on screen and propped on top of a box of crackers, added, "I can't believe you got to hang out with Russell Westwood!"

"I told you he was helping us with the tea shop," Eliza said.

"Well, you're a bad communicator," Mackenzie said. "You made it sound like he waved at you from his limo, not that he was in there painting with you."

Shelby turned to Sheila. "What else didn't you tell us, Mom?"

She sighed, dropping her hands to pick up her tea. It had gone cold during all her confessing, but it was still a comfort. "I think you know it all now, girls."

"Okay." Mackenzie cleared her throat. "We've been talking, Mom."

"Clearly." She smiled. She shouldn't have raised intelligent, independent young women if she didn't want them figuring out when she was hiding things.

"I think the answer is pretty simple, and I speak for all of us when I say this." Mackenzie drew herself up. "You need to sell the house and put the money into saving the tea shop."

Sheila leaned into the phone. "What? I can't sell the house."

"It's a great house, Mom, and we really do appreciate all the sacrifices you made to raise us there."

"Yeah," Emma added, "but you've done it. You raised us. You don't need it anymore."

Sheila smiled a weak smile. "It's our home, girls."

"It can serve a new purpose now. Do you know how much it'll sell for? House prices in our neighborhood went crazy. And it'll help keep Granny in her home," Eliza said, putting her head on Patty's shoulder. "Look at her, Mom. She's helpless. She needs us."

"Excuse me!" Patty opened her mouth in mock shock. "I am not helpless!"

"We don't need the house anymore, Mom. It was home, but only because you made it home. Wherever you are, that's where home is."

Sheila bit her lip, trying to fight the lump rapidly swelling in her throat. Her vision blurred with tears, and she looked down, taking a sudden interest in the remaining blueberry cream cheese muffin.

"Don't be sad!" Eliza said, getting behind Sheila and wrapping her arms around her. "Granny said this can be our new house, and we can have Thanksgiving and Christmas here and –"

"I'm not sad," Sheila said, her voice breaking. "I'm proud of you girls. All of you."

She smiled, finally able to take a breath. It felt like her chest could expand for the first time in weeks.

Shelby and Emma jumped up to join the group hug.

"We're proud of you too, Mom," Eliza said. "You're the best. You know that, right?"

"Well doesn't that look nice," Mackenzie lamented. "I guess I'll take a screenshot. I'm stuck here, alone, watching you all."

"You'll have to plan a visit!" Patty said, picking up the phone. "To your new home, for a cup of tea."

Sheila closed her eyes. The pressure on her chest was completely gone now, replaced instead with a warm glow.

Thirty-four

Though her sisters' visit was brief, Eliza made it count. She took them on a hike along the coast and snapped a picture of the three of them in front of the iconic Lime Kiln lighthouse. Their noses were red from the cold, but their smiles were genuine.

"It's freezing! My toes are going to snap off!" Shelby complained.

Eliza sucked in a deep breath. "Doesn't it make you feel alive?"

"The threat of shivering so hard I lose my balance and fall onto the rocks below?" Emma said through chattering teeth.

"No!" Eliza yelled over the wind. "The cold! It reminds you you're alive, and you can *feel!*"

It was so windy that they couldn't tell if they were catching spray from the ocean beneath them or from the menacing clouds above them. After half an hour, even Eliza could admit it was a bit much. She drove them into town for pizza and a movie, and they both left Sunday night.

The real discomfort for Eliza came on Monday morning. Cold wind was nothing compared to facing reality at the tea shop.

Though they'd been successful in convincing their mom to sell the house to save the tea shop, money was still an issue.

Granny had told her to take out a reasonable salary for herself.

"You're my best employee," she'd said. "I trust you to pay yourself a fair wage."

As flattering as her support was, there was no money for Eliza to draw a salary from. The tea shop wasn't making a profit, not yet.

They were breaking even, and for most businesses starting out anew, that would be great. But for a tea shop that was entering a non-busy season, it was concerning.

Before heading over to the shop on Monday morning, Eliza logged into her bank account to see if she could make it until the tourists returned in the summer.

For the first time, she was grateful she'd been a hermit for the past few years. Her savings were enough to get by, but only if she didn't contribute to household expenses at all.

She didn't feel good about mooching from her grandma and made up her mind to pick up a second job. It wasn't ideal, but she could make it work.

•   •   •

After opening the shop at eight and serving their only customer, she logged onto the website and nearly dropped out of her seat.

There were over three hundred tea orders waiting to be mailed out, and the tea shop email was overflowing with messages.

Eliza started clicking through. "Have you ever considered doing a virtual tea with Granny Patty?" one woman wrote. "I would pay for that!"

The week prior, she'd uploaded a video of Granny showing how to make the perfect cup of English tea. It had only gotten four views all weekend, and now it was up to twelve thousand.

Her mom walked into the tea shop carrying a box of pastries. "Is everything okay?"

"Mom! Look!" Eliza spun the laptop screen around. "We are getting a ton of business and I have no idea why."

Mom set the box down and put a hand over her mouth. "What on earth is going on?"

They scrolled through the emails until they found one offering some clarity. "Is this the tea shop on the island where Russell Westwood lives?"

Her mom frowned. "Do you think someone spilled the beans that Russell lives next door?"

Eliza shook her head. "It wasn't me, but I'm mad I didn't think of it first."

She pulled up a search for "Russell Westwood tea shop" and immediately got ten news articles all repeating the same thing. The one with the catchiest title got her: **Star Russell Westwood Reveals Where He's Been Hiding All This Time!**

The article managed to sneak in five hundred words of nothing before referencing a post on Russell's new website. Eliza immediately went straight to the source and found a video of him.

"Hey everyone, it's Russell Westwood." He smiled, but knowing him in real life, Eliza could tell how uncomfortable that smile was. "I know I've fallen off the face the earth for a few years, but I'm back. I, ah, moved to an island off the coast of Seattle called San Juan, and, uh..." He trailed off, laughing. "Can you tell why I need someone else to write my lines for me?"

Eliza laughed and snuck a glance at her mom. Her eyes were focused on the screen, her expression unreadable.

"I'm re-discovering all the good in the world," he said. "The first place I found it was at this tea shop – A Spot of Tea. It's run by a lovely grandma who is an expert in all things tea and baked goods. Seriously, check it out. Granny Patty is one mean baker, and uh, please stay tuned, I've got more to come."

Eliza turned to her mom, a grin on her face. "I can't believe it! Do you think Granny made him do that?"

Her mom shook her head. "I don't think anyone could *make* him do that."

Eliza kept scrolling through Russell's website and found another video: **An open letter to Lottie the Whale.**

Her mouth dropped open. "Have you seen this?"

Mom shook her head, her eyes wide, her voice small. "No."

"Hey everyone, Russell here. Do I need to say that every time? It seems arrogant not to. Though I guess it's my website." He laughed and scratched his eyebrow. "Well, anyway. I haven't spoken much about my divorce, and I'm not planning on starting now, but let's just say I lost a lot, but I gained some things, too. One of those things was a park called Marine Magic Funland.

"This place – it wasn't something I ever planned to be involved in. You've probably have never heard of it. It's a little park out here with roller coasters and cotton candy and all of those delightful things.

"The park is also home to a beautiful killer whale named Lottie. I didn't know much about killer whales before – I'm more of a wolf guy myself – but it was recently brought to my attention that Lottie is a member of the endangered southern resident killer whale pod, a group who happens to live here around this very island.

"Life is strange and serendipitous. I never knew about Lottie, just like I never knew about the whales in this place I now call home. And while my partners are not going to be happy with me, my plan is to find a way to get Lottie out of our park. I've met a lot of wonderful people on the island, and there are many researchers and experts who believe she can be retired from performing and into a sea pen.

"Unfortunately, that means the end of retirement for me. I'm devastated, of course, but I need to raise the funds to get Lottie into her new place. To that end, I'm going to shoot another movie, and I have a poll on my website where you can vote what kind of movie I should do. All the proceeds will go directly to bringing Lottie home."

He paused and squinted. "Right now it looks like zombie rom-com is winning..." Russell shook his head. "I will do whatever the votes demand, but please don't let a zombie rom-com movie happen. You have until Christmas to get your votes in, so hurry on over."

The video ended and Eliza turned to her mom. "You didn't tell me he was going to help with Lottie!"

Her eyes were wide. "I didn't know."

"Have you talked to him?"

She shook her head. "I don't think he wants to talk to me."

"But look!" She pointed at the screen. "He's listening to you!"

She put a hand on Eliza's shoulder. "I'm just happy things are falling into place."

Her mom turned and disappeared into the kitchen.

Thirty-five

The air in Sheila's lungs escaped so rapidly it felt like her sternum would snap.

The entire time she watched Russell's video, she was frozen, waiting for him to mention her, waiting for even a hint at her existence.

But he'd said nothing. As though she didn't exist and it had all happened without her.

As though he'd entirely forgotten her.

Sheila took in a jagged breath and set the box of pastries down. Patty's chocolate pavlovas and mango cheesecakes had tempted her only a moment ago, but now the sugary-sweet smell turned her stomach.

She pushed the box away and stood with her hands on the sink.

It didn't matter what Russell said, only what he did. And he was doing the right thing – he was going to help Lottie. That was all that mattered.

It was the last thing she'd set out to achieve, and here it was. Why couldn't she be happy? Everything had worked out. Neither Patty nor Derby would be displaced in their golden years. The tea shop would stay open, with a revitalized Eliza running it. Lottie, at last, would get to come home.

Sheila had asked for too much. She was selfish. Who was she to expect more? Had she really believed Russell Westwood would be interested in her?

The nausea passed. She worked quickly, taking the pastries out and arranging them on display plates.

When she carried them out to the front, Eliza was busy with a customer. Another small blessing.

She tidied up and slipped outside to make the walk back to the cottage. Sheila paused for a moment, staring at the vast sea in front of her.

There were miracles in this life, and several had happened simultaneously. But even a miracle couldn't get Russell to forgive her.

• • •

Sheila went back to the cottage and locked herself upstairs to write cover letter after cover letter. What had seemed like an impossible task before was now a welcome escape.

Most of the jobs she'd found were in Seattle, but there were a few remote positions that would allow her to stay and keep helping Patty.

In the afternoon, she took a break to run to the grocery store. When she got back, Patty was waiting in the kitchen. "You go upstairs and finish your applications. I'll make dinner tonight."

Sheila continued unpacking the groceries. "You've been baking all morning. Go take a nap."

"I'm not tired!" she said firmly. "I can lie down while the roast is in the oven. Now go!"

Patty glared at her and Sheila put her hands up. "Okay! Sheesh!"

She'd told Patty long ago that she wouldn't take over, that she was here to help. Though she had no idea why this particular roast was so important, she wasn't going to push it.

Back upstairs, she managed to finish five cover letters and submit eleven job applications.

It felt like a lot, but she knew it was just the start. A friend of hers who had recently left the company told her he'd submitted over three hundred applications before he got a new job.

Only two-hundred and eighty-nine to go.

Sheila shut her laptop and went downstairs to set the table. Cool air hit her as soon as she came down the stairs.

She pulled her cardigan tight over her chest. "What's going on? Is the furnace broken?"

"Oh no," Patty said, waving a rag. "I just had to open the windows. I burnt the sauce and I didn't want the fire alarm going off."

Sheila set a stack of plates down and walked to the window above the kitchen sink. "I don't smell anything burnt. Can we close it now?"

Patty slapped her hand away. "No! Not yet. I don't like any lingering smell. It ruins the meal."

"Are you sure you're not just imagining the smell? Isn't that a sign of a stroke?"

"Burnt toast," Eliza said as she walked into the kitchen and pulled forks and knives from the drawer. "That's an old wives tale, though. Strokes cause facial droop and slurred speech. Arm tingling and weakness..." She paused, looking up. "What else?"

"They can cause a severe headache," Patty said, nodding. "That's what happened to Reggie's late wife, poor thing."

"Since when are the two of you stroke experts?" Sheila asked, laying out the plates.

Patty laughed. "I've been a stroke expert longer than you've been alive, honey."

She was in a feisty mood. At least it wasn't a stroke.

Sheila turned to Eliza "How was your day? Were you busy with all those orders?"

Eliza smiled. "A little, but it was fine. I got all of them to the post office by the end of the day."

"That's wonderful!" Sheila carried the pot roast to the table and, thankfully, Patty didn't protest. She was busy sprinkling crispy onions on the green beans.

"Did anything else happen?" she asked, taking a seat.

Eliza shrugged. "No."

Patty sat down and Eliza never lifted her eyes.

"Why are you being so quiet?" Sheila asked.

Eliza looked at Patty, then back at her plate. "I'm not being quiet."

Something was up. Sheila was about to probe more when she heard what that something was: a melody drifting in from outside.

"Do you hear that?" she asked.

Eliza looked up. "Yeah. What is that?"

Sheila strained to listen. "I think it's a piano – or a synthesizer?"

Patty clapped her hands together. "Oh Eliza! Were you trying out the new speakers again? I told you to shut them off!"

She sat back and slapped her forehead with her hand. "Yes. That must be it. I'm just so tired from mailing all those orders, I wasn't thinking."

Eliza stood from her seat, but Sheila held up a hand. "I'll go turn it off. I've just been sitting on my butt all day." She got up, grabbing the keys off the hook by the door. "I'll be right back."

The punishing wind from the weekend had calmed to a gentle ocean breeze. It was a welcome change. The air was cold, paired with the lonely sound of waves hitting the shore.

The tea shop stood straight ahead, glowing against the rapidly darkening sky. At first, she thought Eliza must've left the lights on, but as she got closer, she realized it was more than that. Something was flashing on the patio, and the music was far too loud to be coming from inside.

Now she could hear the song clearly: "Head Over Heels" by Tears for Fears. There was a year of her life when she'd played this song on repeat for hours. Sheila couldn't help but smile. Had Eliza been using one of her old playlists to test the speakers?

She rounded the corner and stopped her dead in her tracks.

There on the patio stood a black keyboard with a disco ball hanging above it, throwing flashes of light as it spun. Two enormous speakers were on either side, and there on the piano bench sat Russell Westwood in a black leather jacket.

He caught sight of her and leapt from the bench, clicking the microphone to life. He sang along to the chorus, completely unable to hit the high notes but entirely committed to the message. He pointed at her before mimicking ripping his heart from his chest and tossing it over his shoulder.

Sheila stood, stifling laughter, her hands over her open mouth.

"Ladies and gentlemen," Russell said, his voice echoing in the microphone, "the guest of honor has arrived, the beautiful and talented Sheila Wilde!"

She laughed and turned around. No one else was there. "Hello," she said with a wave.

"Let's see if we can get her up here everyone! Let's give her a round of applause."

He tucked the microphone under his arm and clapped.

Sheila shook her head. "I don't think so."

He walked toward her and held out his hand. "I think you know the words."

"I do, but..." She hesitated before putting her hand in his. "Russell, what is this?"

The last notes of the song rang out and silence fell between them.

He tucked the microphone into his pocket. "I needed to make up for something."

"For skipping singing lessons?"

He smiled and took her other hand. "No, but thanks for that."

His hands were so warm. "You're welcome."

"I'm used to people writing my lines for me, you know? I'm not used to having to interpret and express my feelings all on my own. I'm a simple man."

It was hard not to smile, but the least she could do was not laugh at him. "Yes, you've told me this."

"That's why I needed the song." He pulled her closer, gently placing her hands on his chest. "There's no excuse for what I did, for lashing out at you. For accusing you of lying and..." He shook his head. "I'm sorry. I'm sorry I ran away like a coward."

"You're not a coward," she said softly.

He grinned. "Even Wolf 302 managed to turn his life around."

She couldn't help it. She laughed out loud. "Wolf who?"

"302! He was Wolf 21's nephew. They called him the Casanova. He used to run from danger, nap during fights. He failed – miserably. But he changed. He found the courage to change."

Sheila bit her lip. She didn't know why, but these wolves were getting to her. Tears flooded her eyes. "I didn't know you owned the park. I really didn't, Russell."

"I know." He nodded. "Patty set my head straight."

Her mouth popped open. "No. She didn't!"

"She held me hostage in my own home," he said, taking a deep breath. "I had to be very brave to get out of there alive."

She looked up at him and his dazzling blue eyes, the stars emerging behind him like a scene from a movie, and her heart felt like it would swell too large for her ribcage. "I'm glad you found it in you to survive."

Russell smiled. "I was wondering. Do you think you could find it in you to give me another shot?"

"A sequel?" She scrunched her nose, pretending to think for a moment. "I don't normally like sequels but...I think, for you, I could go for it."

"That's what I was hoping you'd say."

He leaned down and she closed her eyes, their breath mingling just as his gentle lips settled on hers.

Cheers erupted behind them, and Sheila spun around to see Eliza and Patty standing there.

"Have you two been there the whole time?"

Patty threw her head back and cackled. "I wish! We only caught the end. Can you do it again?"

Sheila turned back to Russell and whispered, "I'm sorry."

"Take two!" Eliza clapped her hands. "Action!"

Sheila buried her head in his chest. "Are you sure about this?"

He leaned down and planted a kiss on her forehead. "More sure than I've been about anything in my life."

The crowd cheered again as he swooped her down for a movie-worthy kiss.

Epilogue

Eliza got the honor of helping Granny with the Thanksgiving turkey, an honor she would never allow her sisters to forget.

"I guess I'm just Granny's right-hand woman," she said as she carried plates into the kitchen.

"Yeah, yeah." Emma waved a hand. "As soon as I finish school, I'm going to move in with Granny to overtake you as the favorite."

"Ha!" Shelby flipped the water on in the sink. "I bet I could get the crown in no time."

The kitchen was too small for all of them and their bickering, but no one was going to budge, particularly not Eliza.

She was the one who owed Granny the most. The past few months had been a dream – living with her at the cottage and working at the tea shop. Eliza never thought she could be this happy.

Mackenzie bumped Shelby with her hip and managed to grab the sponge. "While you suckers are fighting over details, I'm going to buy Granny a dishwasher and become the real hero."

Granny burst into the kitchen and let out a huff. "Leave all of that! I'll wash it later."

Mackenzie pretended not to hear her, handing a large platter to Shelby to dry.

"Listen, girls!" Granny clapped her hands. "I've got pies at the tea shop and we have to take them over."

"Take them where?" Eliza asked.

"To Russell's, of course," she said. "I didn't tell your mom, but I arranged for a little dessert for us all to share."

"Uh..." Emma narrowed her eyes. "Does Russell know about this, or are we about to crash his family's Thanksgiving?"

"He's the one who suggested it," Granny said simply, pulling on her coat. "Come on!"

Shelby threw the dish towel onto the counter. "Do you think Holly will be there?"

"Of course not," Mackenzie snapped, still scrubbing. "Why would he have his ex-wife at his house on Thanksgiving?"

"She will be," Granny said with a smile. "Let's go, girls. Get your mother."

Eliza went down to fetch her. She was in the basement, blissfully unaware of Granny's plans.

"I have a few options for games we can play," she said, coming up the stairs. "You can talk amongst yourselves and pick."

The girls were darting back and forth, grabbing coats and shoes, elbowing each other and arguing.

"What's going on?" her mom asked.

"We're going to Russell's," Granny said.

"What?"

Granny pulled her coat off the hook and handed it to her. "I made six pies."

"What?"

"Well, we can't very well go over empty-handed! And I don't think Holly made any pies." Granny shook her head. "Everyone ready?"

"Patty. We can't just go over to Russell's."

"Yes, we can. He invited us."

"When did he invite us?"

"When I told him about the pies! You were too shy to ask, so I did."

Eliza patted her on the shoulder. "It's too late, Mom. You've been outmaneuvered."

She sighed. "I guess I have."

Eliza put on her shoes and stepped outside. Her sisters were already halfway to the tea house.

No doubt they were excited to meet Holly and her boyfriend – the celebrities. Eliza was more excited to meet Russell's kids. He wasn't shy about them, telling stories about them all the time. It'd be nice to get to know the people she already considered stepsiblings.

When she got to the tea shop, Eliza realized Granny wasn't kidding. There really was a pie for each of them to carry: two pumpkin pies, a pecan pie, one cream cheese sour apple pie, a cranberry meringue, and lastly, a chess pie.

"I hope it's enough," Granny said without a hint of irony.

Eliza and Mackenzie looked at each other and shook their heads.

"You take the pumpkin, dear," she said to Sheila. "Lead the way."

"I am not going to lead the way!" her mom hissed. "I'm not convinced you didn't make this all up."

Granny giggled. "We're going to show these Hollywood superstars what the Dennet ladies are made of."

They walked single file to Russell's house, carefully stepping along the dark path and following the warm glow emanating from his kitchen windows.

Granny led them to the back door. They were all there – Holly, her boyfriend Toby McFlaren, Russell, and his kids Lucas and Mia.

Granny knocked so loudly that everyone startled and looked at them. Russell grinned, yelling out, "Please. It's open, come on in!"

Eliza hung back, watching as everyone filed in, listening to the *ooh*s and *aah*s over the pies. It appeared Granny had told the truth and Russell was expecting them. He led the group to the fireplace, where six mugs were waiting with hot chocolate.

She didn't know when it happened, but somehow, the Dennets had found a new home on San Juan Island.

Eliza smiled and walked inside.

The Next Chapter

Introduction to *A Spot of Tea*

Wrong place, wrong time...right romance?

When Eliza Dennet unwittingly walks into the middle of a bank heist, all of her quiet plans are stolen from her. Instead of tending to the tea shop and planning her next steps, Eliza is forced to hide away from the gossips accusing her of being involved in the robbery.

Enter Joey Mitchell, a charismatic sea plane pilot with a plan. After the bank offers a hundred thousand dollar reward to find the robber, Joey approaches Eliza with a deal: work together to catch the crook, and they split the reward.

Thrilled to have Eliza as his clue hunting partner, Joey is impressed by her near photographic memory and her attention to detail – so impressed he starts to worry she may uncover secrets he'd rather keep hidden. As Eliza feels herself falling for him, she starts to wonder if he had more to do with the robbery than he's letting on.

As the investigation heats up, will the pair find the truth behind the robbery – and themselves?

A Spot of Tea is the second book in the Spotted Cottage series. Get your copy now and get ready for a fun and romantic tale!

Would you like a Bonus Scene?

Would you like a bonus scene of Sheila and Russell's first Christmas together? Sign up for my newsletter and get a free copy!

Visit: https://ameliaaddler.com/spotted-cottage/ to sign up.

About the Author

Amelia Addler writes always sweet, always swoon-worthy romance stories and believes that everyone deserves their own happily ever after.

Her soulmate is a man who once spent five weeks driving her to work at 4AM after her car broke down (and he didn't complain, not even once). She is lucky enough to be married to that man and they live in Pittsburgh with their little yellow mutt. Visit her website at AmeliaAddler.com or drop her an email at amelia@AmeliaAddler.com.

Also by Amelia...

Printed in Great Britain
by Amazon

41212314R00148